Mills & Boon
Best Seller Romance

A chance to read and collect some of the best-loved novels from Mills & Boon – the world's largest publisher of romantic fiction.

Every month, four titles by favourite Mills & Boon authors will be re-published in the *Best Seller Romance* series.

A list of other titles in the *Best Seller Romance* series can be found at the end of this book.

Violet Winspear

THE NOBLE SAVAGE

MILLS & BOON LIMITED
LONDON · TORONTO

First published 1974
Australian copyright 1981
Philippine copyright 1981

© Violet Winspear 1974

ISBN 0 263 73506 0

Set in 9 on 11 pt. Linotype Times

*Made and printed in Great Britain by
Richard Clay (The Chaucer Press) Ltd,
Bungay, Suffolk*

CHAPTER ONE

IF a hotel could be said to resemble a rather chaotic palace, then this one certainly did, and Altar's heart sank as she gazed around the splendid foyer and saw the candy-twist columns holding up the frescoed ceiling from which hung ornamental lamps on gilt chains.

Foreign voices spoke words that sounded confusing to her English ears, and uniformed boys dashed by with boxes and packages for the stylish guests coming and going through the swing doors. Lifts whirred, bells pinged, and Altar clutched the red leather jewel-case and wondered what sin had been hers that had brought her to a place so alien to her nature, and in the company of a woman to whom she was a personal maid rather than a social companion.

Altar barely had time to catch her breath between the demands, the beauty rituals, and the running of errands.

"Isn't this just about the most stunning hotel of your life?" Amy du Mont gazed around at the deep carpets and the high columns with the avid look in her eyes of a woman who had married money and still gloried in the sole possession of it now she was widowed. It was her avowed ambition to see the *crème* of cosmopolitan society come and go through the portals of the world's grand hotels, and this one on the Costa de Vista Sol was her idea of the very real thing.

"That's it, honey, you hold on tight to those jewels of mine." Amy drew her ermine stole around her ample shoulders and preened at herself in one of the gilded wall mirrors. She looked smugly pleased by the contrast between her own richly clad figure and that of her companion, who wore a straight grey skirt and a plainly buttoned jacket, her fair hair tucked beneath a plain pill of a hat. The widow always insisted that her young companion wear a hat; maybe because Altar's hair was so fair in contrast to her own carefully dyed hair, which was set in waves of brassy gold.

Amy lifted a ringed hand and caressed the sweeping brim of her expensive hat, in which was set a cavalier buckle set with rhinestones. Amy was nothing if not dashing, except that her clothes were such an odd mixture of middle-aged richness and model-girl archness.

Her arch and painted eyes swept up and down the slim and simple figure of Altar and flicked the unpainted face that betrayed a little of what the girl was thinking. "Do stop looking at everyone as if at any moment you expect to be carried off! I do declare, honey, that you're quite safe from any such attack. Latin men might be ardent, but they aren't hard up enough for you." Amy's lips twitched with a malicious amusement as Altar flushed slightly; she knew full well that it wasn't the people so much as the surroundings that her companion disliked. The girl had simple tastes, and the widow was contemptuous of them.

With a sniff and a flounce she advanced to the reception desk of the Hotel Paloma and clicked her fingers for the attention of one of the male clerks, young, smooth-haired and ingratiating.

"I have reservations, young man." Language problems never bothered Amy du Mont, who declared that a genuine fur and an American accent were the passports to palaces.

Once again she was proved right, and Altar wondered if there had ever been a moment in her employer's life when she had been thrown off balance and left dumbfounded by a situation she couldn't handle with sheer effrontery or a ten-dollar bill. Altar admired such self-confidence without being drawn to it. In the ten months she had worked for Mrs. du Mont and travelled with her, she had never felt a spark of sympathy between them. Having been brought up by an adored but impecunious father who had failed to have her trained for better things, Altar had drifted into the job and found it endurable only because the well-off widow liked to travel and thereby made it possible for Altar to see something of the world.

The reception clerk, having taken due note of the ermine stole and the American accent, swivelled the register so that Amy could sign for the luxury suite she had reserved for herself. As Altar signed for her own single room adjoining the suite, she heard her employer asking the clerk if there were any notables staying at the hotel.

"I don't just come to these places for the sunshine and the paella," Amy said, in her rather loud voice. "Nor do I come for the high-priced plumbing and the flamenco music at dinner—" And there with a gasp Amy broke off, and the next instant, clutching her fur stole and her alligator bag, she was plunging across the foyer—and her objective was a man!

Possibly the most imposing man Altar had ever seen in her life, his black brows elevated in astonishment as the widow charged down upon him, causing him to stand at bay between a pair of the candy-pink pillars, looking utterly dark and foreign in a well-cut riding jacket above a pair of buckskin breeches and high polished boots. In his right hand he carried a whip and it seemed to Altar to stir suggestively, as if he might use it to drive off the woman who was heading for him.

"It is you—it could be no other man! The Conde Santigardas de Reyes—why, how utterly thrilling to see you again, Estuardo!"

Altar heard the words too audibly to mistake them, for it had become almost a reflex action for her to follow in the wake of her employer, and she not only heard the dark stranger so addressed, but she saw distinctly the flash of sardonic recognition in his eyes a moment before

7

he veiled them with his dark lashes.

"I never dreamed of seeing you here, Your Excellency! It's the most stupendous surprise and has just made my day." Amy was so excited she was almost stuttering. "I was told by some friends of mine that the Hotel Paloma was famous for its guest list, but to see you here of all people! You do recall me, don't you?"

"Do I?" he said, in such a dry tone that Altar had to bite her lip to stop herself smiling; it really wasn't the place of a companion to enjoy a joke at her employer's expense.

"I'm Amy du Mont and we met in Paris at the apartment of Madame Ziska, the clairvoyant. Everyone who was anyone was there that night, and I was so thrilled to meet a real Spanish grandee. You're keeping fit and well, Estuardo? I must say you're looking—splendid."

There the gush of words petered out, and Altar rather wished for a hole in the floor large enough to hide in. She went hot and cold at the way the Conde looked at Amy with hooded eyes . . . then they flashed to her, taking in the plain way she was dressed, a sort of glitter behind his eyelids as he gazed at the jewel-case which Altar clutched to her bosom rather like a shield.

Altar tensed nerve and body as his eyes met hers, for seen directly they were of the blue called Celadon, used in the rarest of imperial porcelain—blue with green lights —and equally as rare in that face that was utterly Latin in all other respects. As Altar stood there in a silence which even Amy daren't break, he studied her as casually as he might a vase or a pot plant, and determined not to be overawed by him Altar looked back into those eyes that were set at a sensuous slant in his face. Was it a handsome face? Altar wasn't sure, for what struck her was the strength of the bone structure and the hint of arrogance in the features that were as bronzed as fine leather.

"I don't recall seeing you at the mind-reading party," he said to Altar, and his lips seemed to have a mocking

8

curl. His voice was deep and matched his look of foreign distinction. His English was cultured and spoken with an accent that played over Altar's nerves like a strange music not heard before.

"Estuardo, you are droll!" Though he had spoken directly to Altar, it was Amy who answered him. "This is my companion, a young English girl who has been with me just under a year. That most diverting party took place some time before Altar came to work for me, and as if I'd take my companion to a party of notable people!"

"There are notable people who, I believe, take young female companions into all sorts of intimate places." This time the arresting eyes were upon Amy, fixing upon her coyly amused features until she suddenly flushed scarlet and the rouge on her cheeks stood out clownishly. "Yes, I do remember you, señora, but so vaguely that I could not have given you permission to address me as a close friend. I am the Conde Estuardo Santigardas de Reyes and I have control of a fair-sized province in this country, and it is not a place out of a musical comedy. I trust that I make myself explicit?"

"Why, of course, Your Excellency." Amy smiled nervously while Altar silently applauded the Conde for having the nerve to put Amy du Mont firmly in her place. Having met him briefly in Paris she had tried to claim a level of friendship he had refused to accept. It had shaken Amy, but her next remark proved that she was making a rapid recovery.

"I wonder, Your Excellency, if you would have dinner with me this evening? We could get to know each other a little better." Amy stroked her alligator bag, while Altar wondered what it felt like to have such a thick skin that even a reprimand stung but briefly and all that really mattered in the world was to be seen in the company of someone with a title, regardless of any real communciation of thought or feeling.

But this time Amy du Mont had run up against a wall there was no battering down with her flattery or her ef-

9

frontery. "I fear, *señora*, that I have a previous engagement for dinner." The Conde spoke in a voice that matched his look of sardonic power and disinterest in women who flung themselves at his head. A deep and smouldering power, thought Altar, and most dangerous to women who interested him, for he was the sort who could ravish with a glance, or cut with a flick of his whip.

"Then how about luncheon tomorrow?" Amy persisted. "I'm in a strange place and your face is the only one familiar to me—do be kind and say yes to me."

"I can only repeat that I'm all tied up, *señora*, but I feel certain that you will soon know every face in the hotel." With these words he inclined his head, clicked his booted heels, and strode off in the direction of a flower shop set beneath an arcade of the foyer. As his breeched and booted figure vanished through the entrance, Amy clutched her ermine stole with fingernails that gleamed sharply against the silky fur.

"What arrogance!" She tossed her head. "The nerve of him, treating me as if I were on *your* level!" She glared spitefully at Altar, who was always the butt for Amy's displeasure. "I wish you wouldn't gawk at people like a fish out of water, with those eyes that look as if you never get a kind word from anyone. I hope you weren't expecting one from his high and mighty Excellency? You saw him go into the flower shop, didn't you? Well, he's buying carnations or orchids for his latest flame, and I recall that when I was in Paris that time he was escorting an actress to Maxim's and the opera. These foreign notables have a penchant for pretty actresses, and they always give flowers never jewellery. They think it sufficient that *they're* interested and don't waste their money on expensive gifts."

Amy stood glowering a moment at the arched and fragrant entrance of the flower shop, and then she snapped at Altar to order champagne to be sent up to her suite, and in a mood that promised little fun for Altar she made for the lift.

Altar sighed and wished there was no such person as

the Conde Estuardo Santigardas de Reyes as she ordered champagne for her employer and ensured that every piece of expensive luggage was transferred to Amy's suite on the penthouse floor of the hotel. Couldn't Amy see for herself that she had about as much hope of starting a romance with the Conde as she had of lighting a fire with rain-soaked wood shavings? It was ludicrous of her employer to suppose she could flirt with such a man . . . he was a worldly and well-off aristocrat, and *he* did the choosing, not the woman. Altar feared that Amy du Mont was hardly his ideal companion at dinner or elsewhere.

Having unpacked for her employer Altar didn't take very long over her own few belongings, and as she stowed her suitcase in the half-empty wardrobe she hoped that Amy wouldn't spend too many days at this luxury hotel, whose white terraces and gaily striped sunblinds had less attraction in her eyes than a rambling old inn where the plumbing was erratic, but where the smoked ham and the wild flowers were perfect.

Her small room had no balcony, so she stood at the window and stared down at the rear quarters of the hotel and a slightly wicked smile curved her lips. Far down she could see dustbins clustered in a small courtyard, and some bedraggled geraniums in a tub. The luxury of these places was never hers . . . not that she wanted it, for she only sighed for the luxury of being her own mistress. Of having just enough money so she didn't need to work for a rich, self-indulgent widow to whom the title of companion really meant untiring and uncomplaining servant.

Altar shrugged to herself; she didn't have to stay with Amy and could always learn how to be a shop assistant or a waitress. But such jobs didn't have the compensation of boats and trains and occasional stolen hours in lovely old churches, quaint little cafés on cobbled waterfronts, and those tucked-away museums where such quaint things were on display for anyone with a bit of imagination to enjoy them.

These were the things that Altar couldn't relinquish,

and because she had a sense of humour tucked away behind her air of reserve she enjoyed at times Amy's gauche attempts at playing the lady, or the *femme fatale*; that was when the man involved didn't have about him the look of a matador who might enjoy baiting a clumsy bull. A man like the Conde would only have time for a brave bull, or a beautiful woman; of that Altar felt entirely sure.

Lost in her reflections, Altar gave a start as the door of her bedroom was pushed open and Amy appeared, her fur-edged purple negligée rather at war with her brassy-coloured hair. "Why are you standing about day-dreaming?" she snapped. "Come and massage my feet, which are giving me no peace. You know I always need to have them rubbed if I'm to get my afternoon nap."

"Yes, Mrs. du Mont." Altar followed her employer into the adjoining suite, which was very lush and with a wide balcony overlooking the promenade and the sea.

"And close those blinds," Amy ordered, as she lowered herself to a cushioned lounger and kicked off her fur-edged purple mules. "That sun seems as bright as if we were on the Côte d'Azur."

That stunning brightness was reflected off the glimmering sands that stretched along the sea-front, and as Altar closed the louvred blinds she felt a youthful rebellion stirring within her. How she would have enjoyed a stroll along the seashore, beyond that attractive promenade where tall lilac trees were trained into the shape of parasols, with Bohemian glass lamps set inside them. When twilight fell and the lamps came alight, this place would surely be more evocative than even the Côte d'Azur, which was mainly lit at night by the lights of the gambling casino.

But instead of being out in the sun and the sea air, Altar was closeted with this woman who wore high-heeled shoes half a size too small for her, and then couldn't understand why her feet ached when she removed them. Altar opened the big jar of expensive skin-cream and proceeded to smooth it into Amy's feet, which were

12

hardly a pretty sight, the cramped toes all knobbly from the corns which her expensive but uncomfortable shoes induced, with hard patches of skin on the flat heels above the thick ankles.

On a table beside the lounger stood the bottle of Chateau Yquem and the stemmed glass from which Amy had been drinking her champagne. The scent of the wine mingled with Amy's perfume and the skin-cream, and in a little while Altar began to feel slightly sick. She prayed that Amy would soon drift off to sleep, for she just had to get out of this hotel for a short while. Away from this atmosphere of pink carpets, silk cushions and pampered flesh.

It was music of a discordant variety when her employer began to snore against the silk cushions, but for several more minutes Altar played safe and went on gently strok-ing the unlovely feet that protruded from the hem of the purple robe. Rhythmic strokes that kept time with the snores, until at last she dared rise from her knees and tiptoe into the bathroom where she washed her hands until every vestige of the skin-cream no longer clung to her skin.

As she wiped her hands on the roller towel her face gazed back at her from the wall mirror. She smoothed her hair, which was of a silky thickness braided into the nape of her neck at the orders of her employer, so that it left her face with a scrubbed, almost schoolgirlish look. Amy didn't like her companion to be noticeable in any way, and in Amy's company it suited Altar not to be noticeable, and the face reflected back at Altar was so without coquetry that men seldom gave her a second glance.

Yet, to the observant, she wasn't really a plain girl. Her mother had been an Irish beauty and she had bequeathed Altar the wide amber eyes set round by thick dark lashes and arched over by wing-like brows. In her mother, as seen in a portrait of her, those eyes had been wickedly flirtatious and inviting. But Altar's gaze was a reserved one; that of a girl of a very personal sort of purity. Not that she was a prude, for her mouth was not prudish but full and faintly humorous, and at the base of her chin there was a slight indentation that gave her face the shape of an inverted heart.

In the right clothes, in the right setting, with a little cosmetic aid, Altar could have looked rather stunning, but she neither cared nor tried to look other than the obedient companion. She didn't want to be noticed by the men whom he met in Amy's company. She was as uninterested in them as they were in her . . . it was only very recently that she had found a masculine face haunting her mind.

The face of the man whom Amy had called Estuardo, and been curtly rebuked for doing so. He looked as if he could be cruel, thought Altar, recalling the way his unusual eyes seemed to play a blue-green flame over everything he looked at. She gave a slight shiver and decided that she wouldn't care to displease His Excellency!

The sun was still shining when Altar left the hotel for a breath of fresh air, and everything was so quiet as siesta prevailed that she felt her pulses quicken. Only she and a chestnut horse tethered to a tree were in occupation of the entire boulevard, or so it seemed.

Altar crossed the wide road and ambled along by the sea-front, where the sands were so empty and beckoning, but she had only a short time of freedom in which to stand by the sea wall and watch the first tints of sunset creeping over the water that had the look of pure shot silk.

Near the shore were small shingled houses whose occupants had colour washed them so that in the pink and topaz light they looked like houses of candy and sugar, unreal and charming, with every windowsill crammed with pots of flowers, mainly a variety of trailing geranium of a dazzling scarlet with velvety green leaves.

There was something baroque and enchanting about the Costa de Vista Sol when the tourists were drowsed by the sun behind the blinds of their hotel bedrooms, renewing

14

their energies for the evening ahead, when the casinos and restaurants would be ablaze with lights and noisy with flamenco music and the twirling skirts of the gipsy dancers would send out a pungent perfume into the faces of the men who sought adventure, and the dark eyes of slim young gauchos would look into the eyes of women bored by their husbands and restless for a flirtation with a handsome Latin, and many of the men of the warm South were handsome, Altar had to admit, in a way that struck her as being faintly cruel and savage, as if women were meant to be chased and then made to suffer.

It was a pity the way fashionable visitors came to these places and gradually spoiled them, drawn to the excellent beach and the warm ocean as if by a magnet; seduced by the sun and the charm of the people . . . a vivid, surface charm with a volcano smouldering beneath the white smile and the tawny skin.

Altar revelled in the sea air for these few precious minutes, and for some odd reason she thought of the time she had gone to Bayreuth with her father for the Wagner Festival. He had loved the power and splendour of the music and had wanted her to hear the operas in their true setting. "If you know that there are such things in the world," he had said to her, "then you'll not be entirely cast down when life sems a bit of a burden."

This was one of those moments when Altar felt that tinge of magic and romance in the atmosphere of this place, but not to be dwelt upon because duty called and if she upset Amy today there might be no chance of escape tomorrow. Altar had to hoard these moments like grains of gold, and her lips were curved in a half-rueful smile as she ran lightly across the road in the direction of the hotel.

The chestnut riding horse still stood patiently by the kerbside, but the sudden swing of the hotel doors indicated that siesta was almost over and life was stirring again, preparing for the activities of the evening ahead. As the

15

doors swung briskly a man emerged, and he was striding so freely that he had walked into Altar before she could skip out of his way . . . a most alarming experience, for he was powerfully built and he would have knocked her flying if his reflexes had not been swift and his hands quite bruising in their strength as he caught hold of her.

"Your pardon, *señora*!" His eyes flashed over her wind-blown hair, free of the pillbox hat she had been wearing when Amy du Mont had accosted him in the hotel foyer, a few hours earler. "Ah, it's the young lady who is not allowed to go to parties, but just as well that you were not at the mind-reading, for you have large eyes that show their thoughts. Beware! One day that woman for whom you work will have a clever moment and see what dwells in those cat-gold eyes of yours."

With these words and a quirk of a black brow above the turquoise eyes the Conde Santigardas de Reyes released his grip upon her. He untethered the chestnut horse, climb-ed easily into the saddle, and with a farewell flick of his whip he rode off into the raw-gold blaze of the setting sun.

Altar still felt his touch on her flesh and bones as she entered the hotel and crossed the foyer to the lift; as she pressed the button she felt the tremor in her hand . . . that he had touched her was unnerving enough, but what he had said was almost as disturbing.

Was it beginning to show in her eyes that she disliked her mode of employment, or was he only guessing? No, she decided; he was too shrewd and worldly to have to waste time speculating about people. He had summed her up as the downtrodden companion who was secretly rebel-lious, and as he had warned, she had best beware!

It would be awkward, to say the least, if she fell out with Amy and became unemployed in a foreign country, with hardly any knowledge of the language and not nearly enough money in her purse to pay her fare home to England.

Home? There was no such place for her to go to any

more. The house and the furniture had been sold months ago to pay her father's debts . . . dear, impecunious man, and so gallant with it. He had dashed into a burning house and had rescued an elderly couple from the smoke and flames, only to perish himself when he had gone back inside to try and save a pair of lovebirds in a cage.

As the lift swooped to the floor on which Amy's suite was situated, Altar resolved to accept the rather sardonic advice which had been proffered by the Conde. She would hold a rein on her feelings until she had hoarded a bit more money, and then it might be wise if she sought some other mode of employment. The trouble was that her wage was less than the usual rate, for Amy asserted that as she ate and slept in the best hotels she must expect a cut-back in pay. Added to which she had only been trained in companionship to a charming and feckless father, and these days a girl required degrees and certain high levels of education in order to find a really good position in a business firm.

The only certainty seemed to be that if she stayed very much longer under the dominance of Amy du Mont she would gradually become a pale, spiritless shadow, afraid to say bo to a goose, and at the beck and call of every whim of a spoiled woman.

As Altar entered the pink suite, she could no longer be sure if a Latin lord had whispered in her ear, or the Devil himself. A faintly nervous smile touched her lips . . . when she came to think of it, another name for Satan was the Lord of Darkness.

The dining room of the hotel was almost full when Amy du Mont made her entrance, followed by her companion. Amy wore a rustling gown with a train attached, and Altar had to keep avoiding it, almost as if it were a live tail and would cause her employer to yelp if trodden upon.

Altar didn't doubt that Amy would snap at her, for the

17

dress was an expensive one and very much in contrast to the bishop-sleeved blouse and ankle-length, jade-coloured skirt which Altar wore.

Everything about Amy, from her elaborate hairstyle to her jewelled fingers, was designed to attract notice, and Altar was aware of the heads turning as her employer was led by the waiter to one of the most prominent tables. Amy enjoyed being looked at. She liked to give the impression that she had been a famous singer or even the former mistress of a duke. Altar had never heard Amy mention her chain-store husband in company.

They took their seats, and large, gilt-edged menus were handed to them. Altar, knowing in advance that Amy would do the ordering for both of them, let hers lie idle while she listened to the music being played for the entertainment of the diners. The musicians were in exuberant conflict with the chatter and clatter of the people at the tables, and Altar couldn't suppress a smile as she watched a young gipsy fiddling away as if this tourist paradise on the Spanish coast was busily burning.

"Why are you grinning like a Cheshire cat?" The handle of Amy's fan thumped the table in front of Altar; it was an embroidered Spanish fan meant for a more attractive purpose than that of a mallet. "What's amusing you, my girl?"

"I suppose I must be in a good mood." The words came out before Altar could recall them . . . she knew instantly that they sounded impertinent, and so soon after her resolve to be politely demure. "What I mean is, Mrs du Mont, this place seems very interesting. The restaurant is quite crowded with people."

"There's a few too many—it's like Santa Anita in the racing season!" Amy stared with suspicious eyes at her companion and clicked open the silk fan with a bird of paradise embroidered on it. "I well know that you shrink from these smart hotels as a rule, so what has got into you all of a sudden? Have you taken a fancy to one of those gipsy fiddlers? Is that what you're doing, grinning at one of them?"

"Of course not!" It semed to Altar that her employer's reasoning was always based upon the sex motive, and that no man or woman ever did or said anything that was not without a touch of the old Adam and Eve. "I'm not the flirtatious sort, and I was merely thinking to myself that it must be frustrating to be playing to an audience of people more interested in their paella or their roast pork. Such music should be played in a smoky wine cellar, where matadors sit in their dark cloaks and brood on their next *corrida*."

"What a romantic picture," said Amy, looking sarcastic. "So that's what you think about, is it, when I see you looking off into the distance with those eyes of yours, which are far too big for your face! Maybe you're seeing yourself in the arms of one of these moody matadors, romantically scarred from his duelling with the bull. Really, Altar, and there was I believing that you never gave a thought to men. I even began to think that you might be scared of them."

"What have I to be scared of?" Altar gazed at Amy with those clear amber eyes whose lashes needed no mascara. "Men hardly notice that I'm alive."

"True, dear." Amy toyed complacently with the diamond bracelet on her wrist. "You aren't the sort of girl that captures the roving male eye—not that I'm saying you're hideous, but you just haven't that quality of attraction that men find sexy. But it's an advantage really, for a girl in your position. It ensures that you won't be taken advantage of by some good-looking Latin, which would be an annoyance for me—if I had to dismiss you for being indiscreet."

"I'm sure you need never worry on that score, Mrs du Mont." Altar spoke with a slight touch of irony, for little did Amy know that she was secretly planning to make the break from this kind of life, but not with the help of a man. "That kind of folly would be far more annoying for me, for quite honestly I wouldn't give the

19

blink of an eye to a single man in this room, not even if I did have the kind of looks that appeal to men."

Amy raised a plucked and painted eyebrow, and then took a slow look around the dining-room.

"I wonder," she murmured, "where that damnably attractive devil is tonight? Would you give him a wink, Miss Prim and Proper?"

"Who do you mean?" Altar played the innocent, though she knew full well to whom Amy referred.

"The Conde, you fool! That arrogant so-and-so who gave us the cold shoulder in the foyer when we arrived today. If you didn't notice him, then I had better arrange for you to have a pair of spectacles."

"Oh—him," said Altar, and very demurely she watched the waiter set down the *paté de foie gras* and toast which Amy had ordered for herself, and the bowl of vegetable soup which she had ordered for Altar.

"Don't use that coy tone of voice on me." Amy snapped a piece of toast and piled it with the goose-liver *paté*, which as it happened Altar didn't care for. "You know very well to whom I'm referring, and I won't believe you're such a stick of a female that you didn't notice the man or get a thrill when he looked at you with those electric-blue eyes. Strange eyes for a man so otherwise dark—startling, and probably inherited from that grandmother of his. It was Madame Ziska who hit on it; unless she'd been making discreet enquiries when she learned that the Conde was going to be at the party. She said that he had a strain of wild Highland blood in him, and he admitted that his *madrecita*, as he called her, was related to a Scots clan. Madame Ziska was going to say more, but you should have seen the look he gave her when she mentioned a Capitano Draco and his corsairs! The clairvoyant shut up like a clam—well, it's a fact that these high-bred Latins can be as difficult as the devil, but charming—yes, one has to admit they have the grandiloquent charm, and they know how to switch it on and off."

Amy took a deep sip of her wine and ate her way through another slice of toast and *paté*. "It wouldn't surprise me if he had corsairs in his clan at some time or other. What do you say, Altar, and don't pretend the man hasn't made some impression on you, for you must have a few female feelings hidden behind that veil of innocence?"

"I thought him impressive, and certainly a bit arrogant." Altar dabbed her lips with her napkin, for she had to hide a smile at Amy's transparent interest in the man. "But I expect all that arrogant force is bred into his bones and comes quite naturally to him."

"You do, eh?" Amy's fingernails gleamed red as she reached again for her wine glass. "And what would a little nun-like creature like you know about a Latin aristocrat and what's bred into his bones? Have you been doing a bit of historical research? I was never one myself for reading about life—I preferred to go out after the real thing. You deny being scared of men, but I bet you've never even had a boy-friend."

"I was happy in my father's company," Altar said, and she was quite unmoved by Amy's contempt. "I enjoyed his intelligence and humour too much to want the company of some clumsy boy with nothing much to talk about."

"It isn't conversation but kisses that most young people think about," drawled Amy. "I guess being an only child who lost her mother at an early stage you were never as spontaneous as you should have been and developed a shy streak. Why didn't your father marry again?"

"He loved my mother too much." A quiet note of dignity came into Altar's voice. "She had her portrait painted when she was young and still living in Ireland, and I know how lovely and vivid she was."

"But you took after your father." Amy's lips took a malicious curve. "You're the pale and thoughtful type, and I notice you sip your wine as if it were a dose of quinine. Tilt your head and let it go gaily down your throat."

21

"I'd probably choke," Altar rejoined, and was glad of the diversion of the waiter with their second course, tender slices of lamb served with a creamy sauce, baby onions cooked whole, baked potatoes, and green beans. The food looked and smelled delicious, and Amy proceeded to eat greedily, and to frequently fill her wine glass. She liked to think of herself as a gourmet, but was in truth a gourmand.

Altar could concentrate again on the music, which she recognized as a song from *Carmen*, an opera which had been greatly cherished by her father, for it had been a favourite of her mother's. The exciting words spun their way through her mind, asking what was love; asking was it a flame that soon burned out, or was it meant to last for all time, through all pain and all bliss.

"What a blessing this hotel has a first-class chef who doesn't smother everything in garlic and oil." Amy spoke with a carnivorous pleasure that made Altar want to groan. Did her employer never think of anything but her body and what gave it pleasure and satisfaction? Did she never think of music and dreams and what spun rainbows round the sensual facts of life?

"You're letting your food go cold on your plate," Amy snapped. "I have to pay good money to keep you in luxury, so stop mooning about those lean and dashing matadors—who wouldn't give you a second look—and finish that food. Without the good luck to be with me, my girl, you'd be washing cups and dishes in some kitchen, or pushing a bawling brat about in a pram, got up as a nursemaid. Do wake up, or I shall think meeting a real live *conde* has scattered your wits."

"He was far from my thoughts," Altar replied, not quite honestly, for she kept remembering that encounter with him outside the hotel and the way he had told her to 'beware!'

"Then you're either unnatural or a little liar." Amy beckoned the waiter, for already she was eager for dessert. "As there's no sign of him in the restaurant tonight,

22

then I imagine he's dining out with his latest girl-friend. Even if someone like you, Altar, did get a crush on such a man it would be a waste of time. He's the type who likes his women as he likes his cars and horses—sleek, fast, and utterly diverting. A woman would have to know all the tricks of the love game to keep him interested, for he's in a position to choose from the raciest stables and the best families. When he finally marries, of course, it will be to a girl of good family and wealth. I expect she's already picked out and is patiently waiting for him in some secluded convent."

"It all sounds very cold-blooded," said Altar, swallowing the last piece of cold roast potato. "I feel quite sorry for the *señorita*, having to wait around in cold storage while he enjoys himself in the warm arms of other women. Thank heaven I'm a working girl. At least I'm independent of that sort of thing and don't have to be forced into marriage with a strange man. It must be terrifying, even for a girl reared to the idea that she'll marry a man she neither knows nor loves. It's like a slave market!"

"In this case he's immensely attractive, so she'll probably fall for him the first time they're together." A gleam of mockery came into Amy's eyes. "With his amount of experience he'll have no trouble marrying a virginal bride, and his sort only marry virgins—in fact in the old days I believe the bed sheet used to be exhibited for the family and the entire community to see. It was a sort of honour. In my opinion his bride is to be envied. A life of luxury, and a lover like the Conde thrown in! Come on, honey, admit you're envious rather than aghast."

"I'm not really interested," Altar said, and her fingers clenched around her wine glass as she envisaged her own terror at finding herself alone and married to a strange man. "I'm sure if the Conde could hear our speculations about his private life, he'd have something very biting to say to the pair of us."

"He's probably quite used to speculations on his affairs," said Amy, with the superior air of a woman who

23

had been around. She had obviously brushed from her mind that biting reprimand in the foyer earlier that day, and Altar didn't doubt that the moment the Conde showed his arrogant nose in any of the public rooms of the hotel, Amy would pounce upon him and attempt once again to strike up a friendship with him. The very thought of being with Amy when this occurred made Altar squirm in her seat, and she hoped ardently that her employer would soon grow tired of the Hotel Paloma and move on to some other place. Somewhere other than the Costa del Vista Sol, where they weren't likely to see again that man whose gaze was like flame applied to spirit, igniting in Altar the oddest combination of reactions, making her want to flare up, and yet making her wish that like a puff of smoke she could float away and not be caught.

She watched mesmerised as their waiter made brandy *crêpes* at their table, the flame leaping blue and fierce under the silver pan in which the pancake was cooked. There was a scent of squeezed orange and cognac mingling together, and a tension gripped Altar that wouldn't let go of her. She stared at the flames and seemed to look again into those blue-green eyes that had seemed, for a brief and unforgettable moment in the blaze of the sunset, the most beautiful and the most pitiless eyes she had ever looked into.

"Wake up!" Amy rapped the sticks of her fan on the table in front of Altar. "Will you have a *crêpe suzette*, or an ice-cream?"

Altar gave a shiver and dragged her gaze from the blue flames.

"An ice-cream, please." She knew she was meant to ask for the less expensive sweet, but she also wished for the coolness of the cream sliding down her dry throat. She was annoyed by her own edginess, and prayed that her employer would find some other diversion than speculations about a man who was probably contemptuous of both of them . . . the wealthy widow with social pretensions, and the lowly creature who carried for her.

They were having their after-dinner coffee in the lounge, with its cushioned divans, low tables, and the soft glimmer of wall lamps, when Altar felt the sudden grip of Amy's fingers through the thin material of her sleeve.

"Look!" Amy's wine and coffee breath blew across Altar's face. "I'd have bet money that he was with a woman, but what a turn-up for the books!"

Altar, her nerves tightening and her arm tingling, glanced across the lounge and saw that the Conde Santigardas de Reyes had entered the room and was seated on one of the divans—set within an intimate alcove—beside a woman in grey-blue silk and masses of dark sable. The woman gestured with a ringed hand and the gems on her fingers sparkled as they caught the lamplight. Altar tried not to be curious, but she saw the woman's features quite clearly, raised as they were to the intent and impressive leanness of the Conde's face.

The woman had a lovely high-boned face, but it was not a youthful one, even though artfully made up. The Conde's companion was quite mature, but he was being as attentive to her as if she were a radiant girl.

"We—ll, what do you think of that?" Amy hissed the words into Altar's ear. "She's no pretty young actress, but looks old enough to be his favourite aunt. My, there's hope for all of us if his taste in women runs in the direction of maturity!"

It was at that point that Amy's remarks became impossible for Altar to endure. "Please excuse me, Mrs du Mont." She jumped to her feet. "I must see the desk clerk about that car you want to hire for tomorrow. I'd quite forgotten about it until this moment."

Rapidly she left the lounge, leaving her employer to sit alone like some black widow spider gorging herself on scandalous thoughts. There was nothing to be done to stop Amy from indulging one of her favourite pastimes; all Altar could do was not to be seen sharing that awful and intrusive curiosity about the Conde and the lady in the sable cloak.

CHAPTER TWO

THE next few days were given over to sight-seeing, and Altar drove about the Costa de Vista Sol in the limousine hired by Amy and complete with a uniformed driver. They lunched at a table beside the car, from a well-stocked hamper provided by the hotel management.

Like many other tourists Amy was determined to see, if not truly to absorb, the many attractions of this superb stretch of Iberian coastline. Much of it was still unspoiled, to Altar's delight, and there were pretty valleys to be seen, their slopes hung with grapevines. There were farmhouses painted white and looking like the secluded homes of the Moors, who long ago ruled this region. They saw a wonderfully old convent, with cool cloisters where fan-tailed pigeons threw their shadows on the tiles. And a small palace where the vestibule had columns upheld by marble gods and their nymphs.

Amy yawned in the library of the *palacio*, but Altar was enthralled by the collection of porcelain and old jewellery contained in the cabinets with scrolled pediments, almost reaching to the ceiling with its frescoes in jewel colours. The room smelled of history and drama, and she could have wandered there an hour or more, but Amy's high heels were impatient on the parquet floor, and she had her gold cigarette-case halfway out of her bag before they were halfway out of the door.

They roamed in the ancient courtyard, where a tulip tree was rampant with flower, beautiful against the old stone walls, but all Amy had to say was that it was a pity the blooms were allowed to grow wild, for they would fetch a good price in a florist shop. She plucked one of the waxy, petalled cups and put it to her nose, then she tossed it carelessly into the stone basin of a fountain where it drifted like a pink water-lily.

One evening they attended a concert at a castle, and it was there once again that they saw the Conde Santigardas de Reyes with the exquisitely dressed woman whose silver hair this time was veiled in a lovely mantilla of black Spanish lace. This time the Conde noticed Amy du Mont and her companion and he briefly inclined his dark head, but made no attempt to introduce his companion.

The concert of Falla music was spoiled for Altar by Amy's annoyed fidgeting and the remarks she hissed into Altar's ear. On the way back to the hotel she referred to the Conde as a man with a mother complex if he had to go about with a woman so much older than himself.

It seemed to Altar that Amy was behaving as if she and the Conde had once had an affair and she was now being ignored in favour of someone else. It was ridiculous, and Altar wished she had the freedom to tell Amy not to be so vain and foolish.

"I think we'll move on in a day or so." Amy made this decision as Altar creamed her neck for her, working the scented, oily stuff into the thick flesh. "I've a yen to see Portugal and we're on the route, as it were, and it would be amusing to see a friend of mine who lives there in Lisbon. What a girl she's been in her time! Has had four husbands and not a single divorce, and has run through their fortunes like a filly in a field of oats. Yes, I've made up my mind! We'll leave for Portugal in a few days and leave this boring place behind us. I must say I'm disappointed in the coast of the beautiful sun; it's too hot in the afternoons to do anything but sleep, and there aren't that many interesting people staying at the hotel. We should have come when the season really gets going."

Altar could have retorted that if Amy ever took the trouble to take any interest in anything or anyone other than herself, then she might find a lot to like in the

27

surroundings of the hotel. But they never went to the wild and picturesque end of the long beach, nor into the high hills where the wind blew so freely. They never mixed with the local people, only with other visitors at the hotel, and only those who seemed to have the most money and the most self-importance.

"Press more firmly, my girl! The cream has to penetrate deep into the muscles of the neck in order to keep them firm and supple." These orders were flung sharply at Altar, even as Amy reached for a rum chocolate from the big box on the table beside the *chaise-longue*. "Tell me, did you think that woman with the Conde was good-looking?"

"I should imagine she's been a great beauty in her day." Altar fought to keep a composed face, for Amy was staring at her through the mirror of the vanity-table. It was obvious that Amy herself had never been beautiful, but the mature companion of the Conde had the stylish elegance and the fine bones of a woman who would never be other than striking. Altar sensed that Amy was boiling with envy and spite.

"I thought she looked rather scraggy, but the clothes help, of course, for they're obviously made by one of the best fashion houses. She probably has lashings of money and that's why he hangs around her. It's either sex or cash, with his sort."

"When we first ran into him, Mrs du Mont, I had the impression you were delighted to see him again." Altar just had to remind Amy of the initial flap she had got into when she had forced herself on the Conde, claiming acquaintance with him and almost begging him to dine with her. Now like a woman scorned she had turned on him, and in all fairness Altar had to protest against these spiteful digs at the man.

"I've now had time to revise my opinion of him, and don't get insolent with me, Miss Garret! What would you know about beauty and attraction? In all the time you've worked for me, I've never seen a man look twice

28

at you. As far as men are concerned you don't exist, so just keep your mind on your work, and don't be presumptuous because I happen to treat you almost like my own daughter."

God forbid! The words leapt into Altar's mind and she quickly turned away from the mirror in order to wipe her fingers and to hide her eyes from Amy. "Will that be all, Mrs du Mont? You don't want me to read to you—?"

"No—no," Amy waved an irritable hand. "I'm going to smoke a cigarette, and you can go to bed. In the morning we'll start making our arrangements for Portugal."

"Yes, Mrs du Mont. Good night."

Altar slipped away to her own room, where she immediately scrubbed her hands until they stung from the friction of the brush. The touch of that woman was becoming acutely hard to bear, for she had neither grace of flesh nor grace of mind, and Altar sat on the foot of her bed and wondered how she was going to bring herself to go to Portugal with a woman who grew more pettish and uncharitable as the days went by. Amy and her demands were constant throughout the day, and when she couldn't sleep, having made herself wakeful and edgy by smoking in bed, she'd wake up Altar, toss her a magazine, and loll against her pillows while Altar read aloud of other people's love troubles and beauty problems, and fought not to topple out of the chair from sheer tiredness and boredom.

What was she going to do? Altar pressed her fingertips against her eyes and seemed to see imposed on the darkness the lean and humorous face of her father. This was not the kind of life he had wanted for her . . . he would have thoroughly disliked Amy du Mont and called her a selfish tyrant, yet in a way, and Altar realized it, he had been rather selfish himself in not allowing his only child to go and learn how to be a secretary at one of the new business schools for women. But at that time it had not occurred to either of them that his gallant, rather poetic spirit would lead him to sacrifice his life.

They had been happy and content with each other's company, and though there hadn't been a lot of jam on their bread, so long as they had their music and their hikes in the country they had been carefree as a pair of blackbirds.

Altar sighed for the dear times gone for ever, and knew that she just had to face up to the days ahead until she had saved enough money to be able to leave Amy's employ. And when that day came Altar vowed that she'd do anything—scrub floors if necessary—rather than become the companion of another self-absorbed woman.

There was surely no hell devised by man that compared with being a young woman alone and at the mercy of an older woman who held the purse strings and used them to choke all the spirit and initiative out of her employee. Please, Altar prayed, let something happen! Anything that might get me away from this life of painting and primping a faded lily to look like an orchid!

And the very next day, as if in answer to Altar's prayers, some friends of Amy's arrived from America and right away the widow attached herself to the Dawnbergs, and Altar found herself with an unexpected bonus of freedom. Smiling, hitching her pants, she ran from the hotel like a puppy who had happily slipped its lead. She made for the wide stretching beach, avoiding the golden lads and lasses laughing on the sands, her objective the half-ruined sea-tower which she had noticed the other day, as the limousine had driven past the beach and the sea.

At last, out of range of the flirtatious laughter and the water games, there it stood alone, withdrawn and secretive, its dramatic shadow thrown across the stones of the breakwater. Altar's heart beat fast, for she had longed to come here, where seabirds would cry on the roof like cats in distress.

Taking off her sandals, Altar waded through the water to the ledge of rough stone that led out to the tower, and with a sandal in each hand as if to balance her progress she made her way along the ledge until she arrived at the gothic-like entrance into the ruined place. Birds fluttered and squawked and then settled down again, too sure of this place as their own to resent the intrusion of a thin young stranger who trod the winding stairs to the lookout platform, where the guard rail had long since fell away.

Altar sensed that the tower was not the safest place she could have chosen, but she was too intrigued to care that her perch was a dangerous one. Down below she could see the tips of rocks under the silky swish of the water, and there were drifting green tails of seaweed lipping and dipping over the stone as if alive. The air was stung with the scent of salt and old walls limed with bird droppings. Above floated the sun, and Altar felt a sense of joy in being alone where Amy du Mont couldn't find her. Bless the Dawnbergs for arriving to release Altar from what she had begun to think of as her captivity. At least she could get away for an hour or so, to be herself again, and not just the servant and shadow of the Queen Spider, as in her secret thoughts she called Amy.

She smiled to herself and leaned against a broken shoulder of the lookout wall. The sea made its mysterious music, to which the flap of birdwings added a sort of downbeat. It was mid-morning, so Amy wouldn't require attention until almost lunchtime, when she would change into another dress and probably demand to have her hair rearranged. Altar relaxed and felt the sea wind blowing through her own loosened hair, which the sunlight stroked, bringing out the little amber lights that matched her eyes.

For so long had she thought of herself as almost invisible that it didn't occur to her that the horseback rider she suddenly noticed down on the shore would see her own figure outlined in the lookout opening, childish in the distance but for her blowing hair.

She watched the rider gallop nearer, and her eyes shone as he headed his mount into the water so that it splashed the silky haunches. The man and beast seemed as one like a centaur, and because Altar believed herself unobserved she was able to enjoy the display, the way the man rode

31

the horse at the waves, like a conquistador riding down enemies. It was a scene that added to the lonely magic of the place, and then horse and rider went out of sight and Altar was alone again.

Alone and lost in her thoughts until a bird suddenly flapped its wings and flew upwards, and she felt the quickening of her pulses for no certain reason.

She faced the sea . . . the winding stairs were behind her and it was her backbone that tingled and warned her that she was no longer alone. She swung round and her eyes were as amber as a cat's, as they focused on the man who had appeared Altar gave a gasp, as if a hand had caught her by the throat.

The man who had galloped the horse into the sea had been wearing a dark tunic high at the throat, and the man who had joined her on the roof of the tower was clad in the same way, the tunic close and silky against his wide shoulders and lean hips in cord breeches. The heel of one of his boots scraped the stone floor, and a riding whip swung lazily in his hand.

In the bold sea light he looked taller than ever, less the *charmeur* of women and much more the man of action. His gaze was unwavering, fixing Altar to the spot where she stood, the tower opening directly behind her so that if she retreated from him she would fall a hundred feet to the shore.

"You know me so there's no need to look so alarmed," he said. "In fact you alarm me, for one single backward step and Señora du Mont will be without her slave. Move carefully to your left and the solid wall will be at the back of you."

He didn't raise his voice, but there was that in his eyes which made Altar obey him without argument. She drew back against the wall and every nerve and bone in her body was as tensed as if a tiger had loped up the stairs of the tower. His blue-green eyes swept from her wind-blown hair to her startled lips, from the unbuttoned neck of her shirt down to her sandalled feet, poking from

32

the bottom of her nun-grey pants.

"This is the first time I have seen you on your own," he said, a sardonic note in his voice. "Always before you have been attached to the *señora* like a cherry to a jam bun, and always carrying some article or other to the table beside the pool. The well selected table so the widow may sit and watch all the comings and goings, and weave her web of speculation about the various activities of the hotel guests. Tell me, as a young English girl do you enjoy being the fly in her web? You look to me as if you might have tormented wings fluttering wildly to escape . . . . is that why you come here to this rather derelict sea-tower, to contemplate ways and means of escaping from that overpowering woman for whom you fetch and carry and act as dogsbody?"

Altar had listened to him in silence, while her nerves regained their control, and her scattered wits slowly returned. A little wave of rage swept through her as she realized what he had called her. "That isn't very nice," she had forgotten for the moment that she was addressing a *conde* and could only view him as an invader of her privacy who thought he had the right to speak to people any way he pleased. She accepted it from Amy du Mont because she was paid to do so, but she wasn't going to endure it from someone she hardly knew. "I suppose you consider it your privilege to go around calling people a dogsbody, but in England we're a little more polite and keep our thoughts and opinions to ourselves."

"A very commendable national attribute," he drawled, sliding a cigar case from a hip pocket of his breeches and opening it with deliberate movements of his lean, strong-looking fingers. He selected a thin, very dark cigar from the case, and all the time his eyes dwelt on Altar's indignant face with an indolent gleam of amusement in them. Her words had brushed off him and left not a single dent. "But it must at times be very frustrating to have to keep the firm upper lip when you are really dying inside to release all the pent-up fury and passion of your thoughts and opinions. It might be polite, and good for the soul, but it can't be good for the nerves. A while ago you jumped like a cat when I came up those steps, yet you must have seen me riding along the shore. I saw you, *señorita*, standing alone up here like the ghost of a young Ellida."

"Is there anything wrong in liking one's own company —Your Excellency?" She tried to sound cool, even a little insolent, but she only succeeded in sounding on the defensive. In all ways he had the superiority . . . he was of this land and of its ruling class, and he was also a man of the world from the sea-splashed tips of his riding boots to the wind-ruffled raven darkness of his hair. His hand was steady as a rock as he applied a lighter to his cigar, and even the flame would not defy him, for the end of the cigar smouldered at once.

Altar's own hands were gripping the rough stone wall where she stood and she felt at bay, strangely at the mercy of this man who allowed a certain mocking amusement into his eyes but nothing else. The smoke wavered about their magnetic blueness, and the eyelids had a slanting, carved look. His bigness of frame was almost European, but the exotic shape of his eyes gave him away as a man not of Europe but of a province as old, secretive and unexplored as the sharp peaks rising in the distance against the blue and gold sky.

There was snow on those tips and a certain cruelty about their outline, and Altar felt sure that they expressed a part of this man. He looked as hard and strong as they did as he stood smoking his cigar, a booted foot resting on some of the broken wall that had fallen to the floor of the sea-tower. The black silk of his tunic collar seemed to intensify the splendour of his jawline, and there was not a hint of that chivalry which had been so apparent whenever Altar had caught sight of him with the lady in the sable cloak.

The Havana cigar smoke wafted to Altar's nostrils, strong and fragrant, and an evocative change from the Virginia smoke of Amy's cigarettes.

34

"People who are independent of employment can afford to be generous with their opinions and their remarks," she said to him. "I have to work for my living and so it's a case of speech being silver and silence gold."

"I can't really imagine that the *señora* pays you a lot of gold for all that discreet and pathetically loyal service which you give in return." He blew a smoke ring, which drifted blue into a ray of sunlight. "It really is a pity to see someone so young and energetic in the company of that spoiled woman who never walks further than the restaurant, the pool, or the cocktail lounge. Where is she at the moment? Have you smothered her with a silk pillow in order to get a little time to yourself?"

Despite the effect he had on her, that of alarm tempered by a feeling of being very naïve by comparison to him, Altar couldn't hold back the smile that shook her lips. There had been times when she had longed to smother the constant demands and grumbles and absurd vanities that were a large part of her day, and it seemed little short of uncanny the way the Conde could read her mind. Uncanny and disconcerting, for though he might know a lot about women Altar didn't believe that he had had much to do with dowdy companions who lacked the art of being smooth with a man.

"Friends of hers have arrived from America and so I have a little more time to myself and can do some exploring," Altar explained, but she could feel her own tension as she spoke; her wariness that was so in contrast to the Conde's air of being at ease in any situation; hell, high water, or the volcanic eruption of woman or mountain. He seemed unshakeable, and was at the beck and call of nobody, and had all the time in the world in which to please himself. She wanted to look away from him in case he read her thoughts, but his eyes wouldn't let her. He who had command of his own province had command of her, and they both knew it!

He raised his cigar and the evocative smoke from the leaf rolled on the smooth thigh of a dark beauty somewhere in Cuba drifted between him and Altar. An enigmatic smile seemed to play in his eyes as he studied her, a slight tinge of curiosity narrowing his eyelids as his gaze moved with deliberation over her features and found the little dent in her chin.

"You know my name, but I don't know yours," he said. "Please oblige me, for though I sense a little mystery in your make-up and I could think of a *nom de guerre* to suit you, I have it in my nature to prefer reality to romance."

On that point Altar was inclined to wonder; though there was challenge and danger in the Conde's face, there was also a brooding quality that possibly betokened shades of Hamlet and a haunted heart. No man who was the scion of an ancient and noble family ever escaped the past; the old battles and desires stamped his nature, as the pride of the old lords chiselled his features, and the pain of stolen brides left their shadow in his blue-green eyes.

"Don't speculate about me," he said crisply. "I only ask of you what you are named, for the time being."

"Is it an order, Your Excellency?" Altar felt nettled by him, and by the absurd romanticism of her thoughts regarding him. He was hard as the stone of which this tower was built, cold as those icy peaks, deep and dangerous as the sea that swirled about these walls. He knew himself as she could never know him . . . or ever want to!

"I'm Altar Garret, and I have to get back to the hotel—"

"Is Garret your real name?" He ignored the latter part of her remark.

"Of course it is." She gave him an indignant look. "I thought you might have tagged it on to give added pathos to your situation."

"What do you mean by that?" Her amber eyes glared at him. "Are you calling me a liar?"

"Look at it from my angle," he drawled. "Garret—attic —servant girl."

"Oh!" She gave a gasp. "What a terrible mind you have!"

"Women have minds even more terrible, you would be surprised." A smile of sheer cynicism edged his mouth. "It's an unusual name in both respects—Altar, as in worship and vows?"

"Yes." She flushed, for he seemed openly to be mocking her and her name. "You're very cynical, and rather insulting, señor, but I suppose you think your position in life gives you authority to say what you like to—to the underdogs?"

"Very probably." He shrugged his big, black-clad shoulders, and looked unworried by the flaws in his character. "And exactly how old are you, Altar Garret?"

"I—I don't see that you have any right to ask that question," she rejoined. "We aren't in your province, and I'm not under your jurisdiction."

"Don't quibble," he said curtly. "If you were over thirty I should refrain from the question, but I am curious to find out if the señora has robbed the classroom. I suspect that she may have done so, for you have the body, the reactions and the skittish legs of a teenager. Are you seventeen or eighteen?"

"I happen to be twenty, and I'm not staying here to be—"

"Be still and remain exactly where you are." He gave a mocking laugh, and his eyes swept up and down her figure in the plain shirt and the grey pants. "If all English girls were as nervous of men as you appear to be, then it would be hard on the continuation of the race. Even at twenty you are still very young, and it surprises me that your parents permit you to work for the du Mont woman."

"I chose the job—my parents aren't alive any more. And I'm not trying to be pathetic, if you were about to ask!"

"All alone in the world, eh, apart from the widow?" He quizzed his cigar, but not before Altar had seen an odd flash in his eyes. "She is rather like an armoured missile, that one, projecting herself at the desired object with the full force of her insensitivity. I have no doubt that she overpowered you, *señorita*, and made you her victim before you had fully recovered your senses."

It had been something like that; Altar had found herself caught up in Amy's life before she could protest, or change her mind, or dash from the London hotel where she had gone for the interview with the American widow who advertised for a travelling companion. They had been on the boat-train to Dieppe almost before she could catch her breath, and installed on the Blue Train to the *Côte d'Azur* in a dazzling matter of hours. That had been her undoing . . . it was the chance to travel which had sugared the pill.

Now the pill had become awfully hard to swallow, and Altar turned to gaze at the ocean, and she was unaware that there was something a little forlorn in her attitude. The fair hair stirred about her brow and blew in the wind above her pensive profile . . . she had the look of someone who wondered what was to become of her.

"It has not been very long that you have been alone in the world?" The Conde came to stand beside her, and at once she was acutely aware of his height, and the strong grace of his body. He had the supple ease of someone who had no chains to bind him, and he couldn't know what it felt like to be tied to a job. In every respect he was his own master, and the reins of his fate were surely held tight in his own hands.

"I lost my father a year ago," she said quietly, and even yet she couldn't speak of the nightmare way she had lost him. "My mother died when I was five years old. As you commented, *señor*, it's all rather pathetic, like something out of a novel by Mrs Henry Wood."

"Stop that," he ordered. "If you take up cynicism you will find it a hard habit to drop. It would be far better if you dropped the du Mont woman—there are other roads to Rome."

Altar turned swift eyes to look at him, and her startled thoughts were trapped in their amber. "She talks of going to Portugal—it was the travelling that I couldn't resist."

"Quite." A smile flickered on his well-cut lips, but his eyes were thoughtful as he stared down into the water. "The devil lays traps for all of us and we are ensnared before we glimpse the steel teeth. So the city on the Tagus, with its baroque charm and its gentians, is your next port of call? When does the *señora* plan to depart?"

"Soon, I think. Her friends the Dawnbergs are going on to Berlin, where they have a son in the diplomatic service. He's married and has a family, so they'll be staying with him. I should imagine they'll be ready to go by the end of the week."

"Having had all they can stand of the redoubtable widow, eh?" He gave a sardonic laugh and tossed the remainder of his cigar to the sea below. "Do you suppose there is a chance that you could elude her tomorrow evening, so that you and I might have dinner together— not at a hotel, I hasten to add, but at a rather charming place a small way up the mountains? We could meet at seven by the statue in the town square. You could make some small excuse, eh? It should not be too difficult as the *señora* has this involvement with her American compatriots."

Altar heard every word he said, yet she couldn't believe that she was hearing him correctly. He had to be jesting, for men didn't ask her out to dinner—they didn't even notice her existence, and if they did they saw her as little more than a servant, and the kind upon whom her employer kept a strict eye.

It was beyond belief that the Conde Santigardas de Reyes should ask to take her out.

"Are you struck dumb?" he drawled, and she gave a gasp as he took her abruptly by the chin and forced her to look up at him. "Does the widow lock you in your room when she doesn't require your services or your company? *Por Dios,* she would drive me to murder within the hour! Are you afraid of her?"

"No—" Altar's heart was pounding as she felt the closeness of the Conde, and the hard pinch of his fingers. She was more afraid of him than she had ever been of anyone; afraid to believe him when he asked like this that she have dinner with him, and found herself waiting and unfetched at the statue in the square.

"The woman employs you, she doesn't own you." The brilliant eyes stared down into Altar's, as if intent on mesmerising her. "Tomorrow evening you will consign Señora du Mont to the devil, and you will come and dine with me—or are you imagining that it will be you who is consigned to the devil's company?"

"Perhaps I am," Altar admitted. "Anyway, I don't know that I can get away, not by seven o'clock. I have to help Mrs. du Mont to dress, and then I do her hair for her."

"Do you also tuck a hankie in her pocket and make sure she has a penny for a bun?" he drawled. "Very well, we'll meet at eight!"

"You really mean it?" Altar still found his invitation hard to believe in. "You wish to have dinner with me?"

"Yes." His eyes mocked her incredulity, though not too unkindly. "I take it you eat in the normal way, with a knife and fork, and that you aren't one of these food faddists who go in for nut cutlets and mashed turnip, with carrot juice on the side. There are shades of hedonist and gourmet in me, and I admit to liking good food."

"May I ask why you're asking to take me out?" Altar just had to know, for there wasn't the remotest chance that he found her attractive or exciting, and she could only imagine that he was fooling with her, or feeling in the mood for some fun at her expense. Altar hated herself for being so suspicious, but he was no ordinary man, with simple tastes and inclinations. He was extremely sophisticated, titled and rich. He probably had an odd sense of humour, and she was to be the butt.

"Why do you think I'm asking you to have dinner

with me?" He looked down at her, dark and hard and powerful, the sea-blueness of his eyes a concealment, and a jolt to the senses. He could not be disclosed to anyone by reason of his power and his personality, and Altar felt very young and vulnerable in contrast to him.

"I can't think of any reason on earth why you should want my company," she said defensively. "Is it a hoax?"

"My dear child," he said, with a deceptive softness, "are you asking for a broken neck? I could do it so easily, and then toss you to those rocks and ride off, and who would be any the wiser?"

"You're joking, of course!" And yet as Altar looked at him, she wasn't sure, for there was a ruthless quality to his face, and not a vestige of a smile in his eyes.

"You have just asked if I am capable of a hoax, and the answer is yes and no. It rests with the circumstances, and with my mood, and at this precise moment, young woman, I am not in the mood for practical jokes. I could very easily do what I liked with you, for nobody comes to a derelict sea-tower but those seeking a little escape —it would be assumed that you had leaned too far out and overbalanced, and I doubt that Señora du Mont would be more than put out to have lost an uncomplaining maid-of-all-work. After all, who is there to care what becomes of you, Altar Garret?"

"You're very cruel!" Altar gasped. "I thought you might be the very first time I set eyes on you!"

"What I am is no business of yours, and beside the point." He let go of her, thrust his hands deep into the pockets of his breeches and stared out across the water in the direction of the mountain peaks. Altar suddenly observed the gravity of his profile, and the moody set of his lips. He was a man who might be many things, and as he so rightly said it was no concern of hers . . . except that he had asked to see her again, and she was terribly unsure of what she should do. On the one hand he fascinated her even as he made her afraid. On the other he made her feel a little nobody who could be mocked by him because he was a somebody. She wanted to tell him to go to hell . . . she wanted to show him furiously that she had her pride even if she had nothing else.

Her lips were moving when he spoke. "I'm asking that you have dinner with me tomorrow evening, and I am being neither cruel nor kind. If you wish to say no to me, then say it. But if you agree, then I shall expect you at eight o'clock and we will drive into the mountains to the inn. You should like it there. It is secluded and therefore a place favoured not by the gregarious tourists but by local lovers."

Even as that evocative word passed his lips he swung to look at Altar once again, and this time those intense eyes were like the tips of savage sea-breakers. "Your answer, *señorita*!" And it was a command, a click of the heels, a rapier thrust she accepted or avoided . . . if she could.

"If I can get away by eight o'clock—and if you really —" She had been about to say 'want me', but broke off sharply, for there was something erotic about the words, as if she supposed that he wanted to make love to her.

"I do, really." The mockery was back in his eyes, and Altar found it hateful that in her artlessness she was so transparent to a man of his experience. "And now we'll leave this place and you will go ahead of me, taking care on those steps which are broken in places. You will not come here again!"

"Why?" she flung over her shoulder, and the wind blew her hair across her eyes. "Is it your special place and I've intruded?"

"No, but it has its dangers, situated like this at the far end of the shore. What if some other variety of male animal had come upon you? There are devils with scruples, and devils without them."

"Your Excellency," she ran the last few steps to the safety of the sands, "you threatened to break my neck. You said the rocks could have me and there'd be no one

42

to care. I wouldn't call that kind of threat very scrupulous."

"Wouldn't you?" His boots crunched through the sand, leaving large caverns. "I rather take you for a girl who would prefer a broken neck to any other form of molestation—am I wrong?"

Altar pushed the fair hair back from her eyes and regarded his tall figure with a gravity that slightly hinted at a smile. "I don't imagine that you're ever far wrong about women," she dared to say. She turned to look at the sea-tower and saw its isolation, there at the end of the breakwater, with the sea splashing its old, water-worn walls. The seabirds etched their wings in patterns against the sky and she realized that the cry of a girl would sound similar to the cry of a gull and be lost in the wind.

"Have you the time?" she asked. "I—I haven't a watch."

He glanced at the leather-strapped watch on his left wrist, and Altar almost jumped out of her skin when she learned that it was close on lunch time.

"I must dash or Mrs du Mont will be sending a bellboy to look for me. She thinks I hide away in corners of the hotel garden in order to read romantic books—"

"She doesn't dream that you might search for it?" He quirked one of his incredibly dark brows, and though Altar told herself that he was being sardonic, she wasn't entirely sure.

"If I wanted to flirt, or hoped for anything like that, then I'd lay about on the beach in something skimpy." Altar tilted her chin. "I'm like you, *señor conde,* I've found out that romance is a fantasy, and that the thing people call 'love' is just a pair of grappling bodies and a physical greed. I see nothing in all that to run after!"

"No, you wouldn't," he said enigmatically. *"Hasta luego, señorita,* until tomorow evening at eight!"

"Goodbye, *señor.*" Altar flung him a last uncertain look, and then sped away across the sands, leaving him to stroll to where his horse was tethered to a boat bollard, the toss of the reins a jingling music that faded in the other direction until it was lost. He was free to ride to the far ends of the tide, but Altar had to leave it all behind, running from it on reluctant feet until the white shape of the hotel came into sight, poised there on an elevation at the other side of the road. She slowed down and gathered her breath, and did what she could to smooth her hair. She was fairly composed when she entered the hotel, but when she arrived at the suite she found her employer in a rage that she was late, and spent the next hour having insults and hair curlers flung at her.

"Where the hell have you been, and what a sight you look! I pay you to wait on me, not to go gallivanting behind my back. No, I won't wear the mauve suit—" And with a sweep of her arm Amy sent a box of face-powder flying, a pink and scented shower over everything in sight, including Altar.

"Now you can keep busy clearing that mess up," Amy snapped. "You'll have to go without your lunch, and serve you right! I'm going for a drive with Pearl and Sam after lunch, and don't you dare slip away like a cat on the prowl. I want this room looking spick and span by the time I get back for my tea on the balcony. Do you hear me?"

"Yes, Mrs du Mont." And it was then that Altar made up her mind to see the Conde Santigardas de Reyes again. Down on the beach she hadn't been certain that she should, for she hardly knew him, and couldn't really fathom his interest in her. But Amy's behaviour made her feel rebellious, and reckless, and when the door finally closed behind the figure of her employer, she muttered a prayer of relief, which was followed by a groan as she gazed around the suite, which looked as if a gale had swept through it.

Altar felt as if she had gone through the wars in her effort to send Amy off to lunch looking a smarter fashion plate than Pearl Dawnberg, and she wondered what the Conde would think if he could see her right now, face-powder all over her hair, perspiration making her shirt cling to her skin, and dark lashes blinking fiercely to hold back the tears. It wasn't pleasant being sworn at by a woman who cared for nobody but herself, and who thought that her possession of money gave her a licence to rant and rave at a mere girl because she happened to be a few minutes late in attending to the task that had not been specified when she had taken on this job all those months ago in London.

An ache of the spirit had hold of Altar as she began to clear up the expensive debris, and to put away the discarded clothes in the wardrobe. What did the Conde want with the likes of her? It would be intriguing to find out, and she no longer cared very much that it might also be rather dangerous.

CHAPTER THREE

THE odds against Altar getting away to meet the Conde were tremendous, for that very day Amy decided to arrange about their journey to Portugal, and Altar was kept busy for hours with the packing. As her employer travelled with an extensive wardrobe of day and evening clothes, not to mention a separate trunk of shoes and boxes of hats, the sun was dying outside the windows when Altar's task was finally completed.

Not that the completion of the packing set her free, for Amy had a list of travel pills, digestive tablets and skin creams for her to fetch from the hotel pharmacy, and she also had to call at the reception desk to ensure that the clerk had arranged their train booking all the way through to Lisbon. It was a nuisance, grumbled Amy, that there wasn't an airport in the locality, but so long as she had a first-class compartment on the train then she would have to make the best of things.

Her friends the Dawnbergs were leaving after dinner that evening, and Altar suspected that Amy had hoped to be invited to go along with them. It would have delighted her to stay in one of the Embassy houses in Berlin, but it came as no surprise to Altar that the invitation was not forthcoming. A little of Amy went a long way, and Altar could only wish that like the Dawnbergs she was free to go speeding away on the overnight express, comfortably independent in one of those spacious, almost lushly Victorian compartments with tassels on the cushions.

Amy was spending this last evening with her fellow Americans and though eager for the farewell party down in the cocktail lounge, she wanted to look her best, and it took Altar well over two hours to accomplish the task. It was almost seven-thirty when she put the final touches to Amy's hair-do and fastened with tense fingers the diamond necklace her employer was wearing, with matching eardrops that sparkled like small chandeliers against her powdered neck.

Amy stared at herself in the mirror, then with a complacent smile she turned to Altar with a rustle of expensive fabric. "You can have your meal in the cafeteria," she said. "Sam Dawnberg always seems to think that you should sit with us, but I know how out of place you feel in one of those dull dresses of yours. I feel very glamorous myself tonight, added to which I'm looking forward to a change of scene; and Portugal is the most charming place, so long as you stay out of their politics and mix with your own friends. This has always been a rule of mine, for you'll notice that the Latins themselves cling together." Amy took up the scent spray and puffed another cloud of perfume over herself. "There, I'll knock out all their eyes tonight! You did make sure to post my letter to the Senhora Fonseca—my friend Amanda? What a girl! I wonder who she has her eye on for the fifth husband?"

"I posted the letter just before six o'clock, Mrs du

Mont." Altar strove not to glance at the clock as she spoke, for every dwindling second seemed to toll the death of her own evening out. The Conde wasn't the sort of man to wait for a woman, and there now seemed little hope of her getting to their meeting place on the stroke of eight. It was curious that her heart felt so heavy, for up until now she had believed that it might come as a relief if she couldn't keep her appointment with the Conde.

"Don't forget to have my jewels relocked in the hotel safe before you go to the cafeteria," Amy said sharply. "And if you've nothing to do after you've had your meal, then you can come back here and iron that lace blouse of mine. I'll travel in it tomorrow, with my purple suit." And so saying she rustled her way to the door and departed from the suite with the air of a woman supremely confident that she would never have to iron numerous lace frills on someone else's blouse.

As the door closed behind her, an exhausted little shiver ran through Altar. What was the use of getting ready? It was now twenty minutes to eight and by the time she had showered, dressed and done something to her face and hair, that sleek and steely Spaniard would be on his way to the mountainside inn without her. She pushed the tousled hair from her eyes and saw in her imagination that dark and sardonic face, in which the turquoise eyes were as startling as gems against brown velvet. She even had to see about getting Amy's jewels locked away for the night . . . oh, what was the use? She'd dash to the statue in the square only to find stone eyes looking down on her.

Yet, being young and still hopeful despite the odds, Altar recharged her almost exhausted energies and dashed into the bathroom, scattering her clothes as she ran. She snatched her showercap from the hook, and took the water cold and needling on her bare white skin. She needed to rouse herself from the lethargy into which all that packing had plunged her, and she also felt the need to be fresh again after handling all those highly scented

47

garments. She felt as if the scent and traces of body-powder clung to her own skin, and she liked the tingling of her own body when she turned off the shower and quickly dried herself, throwing on handfuls of the light cologne talcum that she preferred to the expensive brands used by her employer. Amy could never accuse Altar of using her toiletries, for they were far too lush and redolent of the boudoir.

Hastening into her bedroom, Altar took fresh lingerie from the drawer and flung open the closet where her simple range of dresses still hung, not yet packed, for they would not take long to throw into a suitcase.

The linden-green with the tapestry hem was about the nicest dress she owned, and one she rarely wore, though she liked it. It belonged to the old days, to those musical evenings with her father . . . there was nothing very fatherly about the Conde Santigardas de Reyes, but all the same Altar slipped into the dress and saw again how kind it was to her skin and her hair. Its simple lines suited her, the deep tapestry hem of varying colours blending with her personality, which was slightly out of touch with the permissive trends of the modern girl.

She brushed her hair and swiftly looped it to the crown of her head, where she secured it with a tortoise-shell slide. Her slim neck and slightly hollowed temples accepted the style, and tonight she powdered her nose and lightly coloured her mouth.

Well, she had made the effort to dress for the meeting, but she didn't hold out much hope that this particular *charmeur* would be patient enough to wait for Cinderella.

Across from the rear of the hotel, where a clock tower arose from the rooftops, there came the sound of the medieval clock striking notes that seemed to declare: 'Too late, too late! The Conde won't wait!' And as if actually hearing those words Altar flung a fringed scarf about her shoulders and ran from the suite . . . quite forgetting that the red jewel-case lay on the bed, its niche of drawers stuffed with rings and bracelets and brooches, and other

48

items, all set with real gems, for Amy du Mont was too shrewd to travel without real jewellery, that most negotiable asset. "Who knows," she was wont to say. "The world might go to war again and I don't plan to be stranded in some foreign country without some valuables I can exchange for cash."

Altar arrived breathlessly in the town square, and it was only then that the realization struck her that she had forgotten to have the jewel-case locked in the hotel safe. Oh, heavens, should she dash back and ensure that the jewellery was safely locked away? If anything happened to it, if there was a fire or a thief got into the suite, she'd be bound to get the blame . . . but even as she stood hesitant the sound of a motor horn blasted the silence of the square, where the moonlight fell upon the statue on its stone platform and made it seem a ghost.

Altar whirled about and there in front of the tall, rather medieval-looking buildings, its bodywork gleaming in the light of the moon, was the large open car presumably owned by the Conde. Again its imperative horn summoned her, letting her know that the driver was impatient. The very fact that the Conde had waited fifteen minutes for her was enough to make Altar forget the precious jewel-case, and catching at her skirt she ran across the cobblestones to the side of the car, the moonlight playing over her hair and her face, so that she seemed a trifle unreal, elusive as a ghost herself in this place that time had not yet altered.

She paused with a breathless gasp beside the car and saw at once that the silvery machine and the dark-browed man suited each other, and her heart was beating in her breast like a tiny hammer as she gazed at him there behind the wheel, his profile looking coin-stamped, as if chiselled by a fine hard blade, and none too kindly, though he had waited for her.

"Come round to the other side of me." The door clicked open. "Place your scarf over your hair so the wind won't disarrange it. It feels good driving into the mountains

49

with the top open."

Altar entered the car and felt the comfortable give of the seat. As she covered her hair with her scarf a dark-clad arm came like a bar across her body and the door clicked shut. She was alone with him, and his eyes glinted as they took her in.

"I assume that the *señora* has been more demanding that usual, eh?"

"Yes—we're leaving for Portugal in the morning." Altar heard the shake in her voice and she blamed it on the skirmish of a day through which she had lived. "I've been busy packing her clothes—it grew so late and I felt sure you wouldn't wait for me."

"Knowing the woman for whom you work I felt it only fair to wait." With his arm still stretched across her slim figure the Conde ran his gaze over her face and her upswept hair under the flimsy silk covering the scarf. "You don't look like a girl who is rapturously eager to leave Spain—there is something pensive in your eyes, and there was a catch in your voice when you spoke just now about leaving. You don't want to go, *señorita*?"

"I have no choice, *señor*. What I want doesn't come into it." Altar tried not to show how disturbing it was to have him leaning close to her, so that the moonlight flung the shadows of his lashes on to his skin, from which stole the faint tang of a male cologne mingling with the fragrance of expensive leather which had often absorbed the smoke of his cigars. He confused her, and excited her nerves in a way she had never known before . . . they had so little in common, and yet here they were together in his car and he was putting into words what had been going through her mind all day . . . she didn't really want to leave Spain . . . her main wish was to get away from Amy du Mont, and it seemed too hopeless to be granted.

She could feel how easy it would be to throw aside pride and admit how unhappy she was, but in that in-stant he drew away his arm and started the engine of the car. It swept around the bend of the square into the road that led away from the sea front; shadows and moonlight flickered over them as they drove along.

"You managed to slip away without exciting the *señora*'s suspicions?" There was a glint of gold at the Conde's white cuffs, and Altar noticed how lean and shapely his hands were upon the leathered wheel of the car, sun-dark almost as the leather, well-cared-for without being foppish. He wore a ring on the small finger of his right hand, which had a tiny eagle stamped into the golden face of it.

Altar felt her heartbeats as she sat there beside him . . . this man had some obscure reason for asking her to dine with him, for she refused to believe that he had any amorous interest in the insignificant companion of a woman whom he obviously disliked. Nor was he the kind to take pity on a girl . . . he would despise that emotion and think it weak.

"Mrs du Mont thinks I'm in the hotel cafeteria eating a modest meal, after which I have orders to iron her lace blouse, the one with about four dozen frills on the bosom." Altar smiled slightly. "You have no idea what I'm risking to dine with you, Your Excellency."

"My dear Miss Garret, you are risking even more than you are aware of," he drawled, handling with aplomb the turning of the car on to a corniche road that wended its way into the mountains, which were mantled with a shrub that gave off a wild herby scent which the night wind blew into the car. Altar took a deep breath of the tangy air and wondered just what the evening held in store for her. Her fingers reached for each other and she asked herself what kind of madness had possessed her to risk Amy's temper in order to be with a man who looked such an enigmatic devil.

The touring car took the gradient with smoothness and silence, and when Altar glanced from the side of her seat she saw far below the lights of the sea-front and the hotels, like golden bells strung upon an invisible chain,

51

and there like a dark finger pointing at the moon the
sea-tower where she had let herself be talked into this . . .
this assignation. With her nerves and her deepest instincts
she seemed aware that this man had some ulterior motive
in asking her to dine with him at a secluded inn where
guests from the Hotel Paloma would not be likely to see
them together.

"What do you think of my car?" he asked her. "Quite
smooth, eh? The English can hardly be bettered for the
excellence of their engineering, the beauty of their country-
side, and the fine complexions of their women. I was edu-
cated in your country, at a barracks called Eton, and
later on I went to Sandhurst for my military training.
There are Spartan instincts in the British, eh? Their great
houses seem always to be cold, and their cheese is always
so hard. You come of a fascinating enigma of a race, do
you know that? Brave fighters but aloof lovers, who
guard their hearts so fiercely that one would think that
a heart was just a machine to run the body."

"Perhaps the British have grown like a rose and feel it
wise to shelter themselves in thorns," she said. "We are
a prickly race, Your Excellency."

"Indeed! I wonder if you could possibly try calling me
Estuardo?"

"Not possibly!" She felt almost shocked by the idea
of being so—so intimate with him. "I hardly know you
—and it's all so fantastic, as if I'd stepped through a
screen and found myself in the cast of a play. I keep
wondering if that moonlight on the mountains is real. Are
you real, or am I dreaming?"

For answer he took his left hand briefly from the wheel
and with a slightly cruel smile he pinched her earlobe
with his fingers. "This is no play, Altar in wonderland,
and I am no actor in a drama written by some effete person who knows more about tin wit than real life. That
moon up there is as real as I am."

His touch was even more convincing than his words,
for his fingers had sent a tingle radiating all down the

side of her bare neck, running like the tip of a flame into the rib-cage that held her fast-beating heart. Oh heavens, was she such an untouched little fool that she was going to get foolish over this man?

"Can't you think of yourself as a friend of mine?" he asked, with mock seriousness.

"Friendship has to grow," she said, speaking with a touch of primness because he had made her tingle and such a sensation surely had nothing to do with friendship. "It doesn't spring full-blown from a couple of casual meetings. It isn't a fair-weather flower, *señor*, and taken all round this is an impossible situation. Take me back to the town square, please! I'm more at home eating egg and chips and ironing Mrs du Mont's blouses!"

"Now don't get temperamental," he chided her, "or I shall begin to suspect that you aren't entirely the English Miss. Furthermore I never turn back once I have set my course. Relax! You are behaving like a cat on thorns."

"That's how I feel—"

"In my car, which is upholstered in the finest cow leather? You may insult me, Altar Garret, but not my beautiful machine. How dare you!"

"How I've dared to come this far I shall never know," she retorted. "Take me back before Mrs du Mont finds out I've played truant."

"Once you dare to play truant you have to pay the price." As he spoke he swung the car smoothly around a bend of the steep road, and there ahead of them gleamed the lights of the inn, music drifting from the interior.

They drove into the forecourt and as the car came to a standstill Altar sat there a moment absorbing the scented stillness which the drift of music intensified. She knew without looking that the Conde's mouth was edged by a sardonic smile. He was too used to having his own way to ever consider not having it, and so here they were high above the coast and isolated from the well-off tourists eating their paella under the gleam of chandeliers instead of the peaks of the mountains.

Altar opened the door beside her, but when she stepped from the car the Conde was there and it was he rather than the uneven stones of the forecourt that caused her to stumble in the high heels she didn't usually wear. He caught hold of her and held her for a breathless moment against the smooth material of his dinner jacket. His hands were as strong as they looked, holding her with an expert ease that didn't bruise and yet gave indication that she would only be released on his terms.

"Take care, Altar Garret," he murmured. "A stumble can so easily lead to a fall."

"It's these heels—" Her voice shook and betrayed her awareness of the double meaning in his words, but she also knew that if she tried to pull away from him she would only induce him to torment her.

"So tonight's glamour is in my honour, eh?"

"I am sure that you are more amused than honoured, Your Excellency!" And how suitable was the appelation, for even in her high heels she didn't measure to his deeply dented chin. She thought of what Amy du Mont had said, that his grandmother had been related to a Scots clan, passing on to him through her blood line the arrogant height and strength of the Highland races. A quiver ran all through Altar, for she felt that he possessed a power that could have broken her like a doll.

"Why should I be amused?" His eyes played over her in the moonlight. "You have a certain fey charm and the touching gallantry of youth that even the wealthiest of women cannot buy. It is the glamour alone that can be bought by them, and I am sure that in her heart—if she has one—the du Mont woman envies your slim catlike grace and your cat-gold eyes—somewhat unusual eyes for an English girl."

Altar listened to him in a sort of daze, for no one had ever said before that she had charm. "My mother was Irish," she said, and told her foolish heart not to be seduced by him. He had a way with women and a dangerous way with words, and she had been lonely for a long time

54

now. She stood between his hands like a robot and did all she could to school her face into a polite mask. "But as it happens I take after my father and love things like music and books. My mother was spirited and a bit of a flirt, and I am a total contrast to her—my father often said so. He told me her eyes were those of a wild hawk, and that mine are those—" Altar broke off and bit her lip. "Oh, it was nothing—a private joke between us. We were very fond of one another."

"Of course," said the Conde, "but you don't intend that I should share the little bit of nonsense about your eyes. Could he have been quoting Wilde, I wonder?"

Altar gazed startled at his dark, sardonic face; he could surely know nothing about her beyond that she worked for a woman he had met briefly at a party in Paris a couple of years ago. It was just that he was wordly and clever at throwing out hooks that caught her in vulnerable places.

"Well," he quirked a black brow, "have I hit the mark?"

Altar was going to deny that he had, but he was far too clever to believe her. He made her feel . . . at his mercy . . . as if he had some hold over her.

"Who—did the mind-reading at that party?" She tried to speak lightly but couldn't quite control her shaky voice. "I should imagine it was you rather than Madame Ziska."

Amusement glinted in his eyes. "You are really too young to have any mystery that I couldn't fathom, Altar Garret. As a matter of fact I thought of those lines of Wilde the second time I saw you, when you ran into me outside the hotel. I thought at once . . . *this curious cat, with eyes of satin rimmed with gold.* Such a pity that you have no Chinese mat to lie couching on."

"I have little time for couching on Chinese mats, Your Excellency." And there she caught her breath as his hands tightened painfully and she was all but lifted off her feet and shaken.

55

"You will not call me that, do you hear?" His gaze was a blue-green consuming flame, and her slight body felt crushed against his powerful frame. "Not because I want you for a friend, but you aren't my lackey, and you are about to eat dinner with me. You say 'Your Excellency' once more to me and you will find yourself in trouble. Now come! We are already rather late and our champagne will be stiff in the bottle instead of pleasantly iced."

She was led into the inn, where at once the manager was bowing to him and almost strutting with pleasure as he led them not to the main dining-room but to a private room, curtained, discreet, and lit softly by shaded lamps, with a spray of mixed flowers scenting the air.

A nerve pulsed in Altar's throat as she noticed the cushioned divan that lay in the shadows just beyond the circular table laid for two. The faintness of the music had an evocative sound, muffled as it was by the velvet curtains that screened the Conde and herself from the eyes of the curious. The bottle of champagne gleamed and waited in the silver pail, and her legs felt weak as water as she sat down in the chair that was pulled out for her.

"As Your Excellency ordered, champagne of the best vintage, and salmon cutlets fresh caught from the lake this very day." The *maître d'hotel* stood stroking his hands together like a praying mantis, and Altar could only gaze speechlessly at him and wonder what his manner would be like had she walked into this velvet-hung room on her own. As it was he was totally concerned that his waiters should do everything to perfection. The cork was pulled with a sibilant, drunken gasp from the neck of the wine bottle and the bottle was cradled in a snowy napkin as the long-stemmed glasses were filled. Silver tongs glinted in the lamplight as the cutlets of moist pink salmon were laid on the white plates with the care and reverence of acolytes at a holy rite. Brown bread, butter and sauces were brought to the table. Sprigs of watercress, rounds of

56

tomato, and stems of celery were left within easy reach of the diners' hands. A murmur, a scrape of heels, and soft rattle of curtain-rings, and the *maître d'hotel* and his waiters were gone.

"I hope you like salmon." The Conde held the bowl of his wine glass cupped in his fingers, and he was looking across at Altar with a wicked, knowing gleam in his eyes. "I took the liberty of ordering our meal in advance, for a place like this usually caters to couples who are more interested in each other than in what they eat and drink. Well, Miss Garret, I drink to you in daring to defy the redoubtable Señora du Mont. What a good thing she is not the mind-reader, otherwise she would be having a pink fit to see you sitting here with me."

"More likely a purple one." Altar had to smile, for she wasn't expected to accept invitations from the hotel boot-boy, let alone the most distinguished guest staying at the hotel and she knew that Amy's fury would be highly inflammable should she learn of this supper for two in a private room in a picturesque inn perched on a spur of the Spanish mountains. Greedy curiosity would then follow the indignation, and this time the Conde would be called a cradle-snatcher.

"I am glad you smile, but you are still so unrelaxed. Come, drink your wine and eat your food, and stop wondering if that divan is there so that later on I can seduce you in comfort among cushions and soft lights." There were wicked lights in his eyes as he spoke and started on his salmon cutlet. "Tell me, Altar, have you always been so afraid of men?"

"Not men in general," she denied, having sipped the wine and felt it run warm and intoxicating through her veins. "I'm just not used to dining out with notables— or with anyone except Mrs du Mont, when she's hard up for company, and you could never be hard up for anything, could you, Your Excellency?"

"I warned you, Altar!"

The words struck with a deceptive softness that made

her flinch. "I know—I'm sorry. I must seem an awful stick and a fool to you. Not much of an amusement—"

"Do you really think that I invited you here in order to use you for my amusement?" His brows made a black thunder above the lightning of his eyes, and his features had a sudden cruel hardness, as if he might rise to his feet and toss her out of sight. "If I want to laugh I go to the cabaret, and when I am in the mood to make love to a woman I don't select a silly little virgin with no idea of what sensuality is all about. Yes, you are a little fool if you think I find you either funny or fetching. You have a thousand things to learn about men, and a thousand more to learn about being a woman."

Then, with a raking movement of his hand, he reached for his wine glass. "For heaven's sake, do I see tears in your eyes? Are you disappointed that I'm not going to round off the meal with your ravishment?"

"No—it just seems to me that people like you, and Mrs du Mont, seem to get pleasure out of waving whips over people like me, just because I work for my living and haven't met anyone to care about me. I—I might not be all right for kissing, but I certainly make a convenient whipping-boy, and as a *conde* you probably had one of those and now find yourself in need of a new one!"

His eyes dwelt intently on her young, hurt face in the lamplight, and then abruptly he towered to his feet and strode round the table to where she sat. "To hell with this!" His hands closed hard and possessive on her slim shoulders. "It isn't a whipping-boy that I need, but a wife, and that is why I brought you here tonight. I thought the inn conducive to a proposal of marriage, and I planned to make your head swim with champagne and charm. But the best laid plans don't take into account the personality of people, and perhaps I am guilty of thinking of you as a shy young fool who could be easily won over. Instead you fight me and assert your right to be thought of as a person and not a puppet. You must forgive me, Altar, for taking you for granted. But you must also take

58

my word for it that this is no game . . . I am asking you in all seriousness to be my wife."

To say that Altar sat stunned would be putting it mildly . . . she felt his hands on her shoulders, breathed the aroma of food and wine, yet nothing seemed real . . . she and the Conde and their surroundings had taken on the aspect of a wild and impossible dream.

"What is it, Altar?" His fingers came to the sides of her neck and he tilted back her head so that he was looking down into her eyes. "Do you think I have gone crazy, or that you have? Poor child, you do look as if you find yourself alone with a madman!"

"Who wouldn't think you mad," she gasped, "to ask someone like me to marry you? I'm not the sort men marry, and *condes* marry girls who are specially chosen for them, titled, lovely, out of convents! Please, my neck feels as if it will break!"

"Better your neck, little one, than your heart." He let go of her and resumed his seat at the table. He took up his fork and began to eat his salmon as calmly as if he had just remarked on the weather. "A marriage in which the two people involved make no pledges of eternal love and loyalty can never break the heart when those pledges are broken, and inevitably they are, people being what they are."

"How cynical of you to say that!" she exclaimed. "Is that what you truly believe?"

"I fear so." His drawl was magnified, as if to impress upon her the extent of his cynicism with regard to the state of matrimony. "Come, eat your food, Altar. I hope I haven't taken away your appetite with my proposal?"

"As if I would take you seriously, anyway." Yet Altar ate her food without really tasting how delicious it was. She felt she had to be the victim of some kind of mocking joke, and yet there had been no mockery in his look, only a sheer intensity of purpose, a compelling quality in his very fingertips, taking possession of her, demanding that she submit to what he asked.

"What next, I wonder?" She tried to be flippant. "Will it be off with my head for calling you a cynical person?"

"It would have been at one time," he rejoined, and he gazed at her with half-veiled eyes, tiny, dangerous lights flickering behind his dark lashes. He tore brown bread and used the butter knife, and Altar noticed the masculine beauty of his hands in the lamplight . . . her heart beat fast and she knew that she was fighting the subtle attraction of the man. *Un prince charmant*, saying things that bore no relation to reality; playing a subtle game with her in order to enliven his jaded sense of fun. She would play along; let him see that she wasn't quite as naïve as he obviously thought her.

"I suppose, *señor conde*, you are giving me a memory to live on for the rest of my dull days? When I'm a middle-aged spinster sitting at my tatting I can look back and nostalgically tell myself that once in a land called Iberia a dashing scion of an ancient and noble house took me to supper at a romantic inn and made pretend that he would like to marry me. I'm very grateful, for the mists of time are bound to cast a happy haze over my mind and I might almost believe that such a proposal was made in earnest."

"*Señorita*," he lifted his wine glass with a menacing grace of movement, and now his eyes were as coldly brilliant as diamonds, fixing themselves on the tiny mole against Altar's left temple, bared by her hair snaked around the crown of her head, "we must all of us dream, suffer ordeals, and face damnation or heaven, and you had better believe that your moment has come to slip those chains that a rich and selfish woman is binding around you. Whatever sort of man I am, I can never be quite so terrible as a self-absorbed widow bent on destroying your youthful anticipation in tomorrow and the day after tomorrow. I want the fact of you, the slim physical female that you are, and I shan't stamp on your spirit with the heavy feet of a woman who hates youth because her own has gone and can't be recalled or truly replaced by the

60

beauty salons."

He drank his wine, his eyes steady upon Altar's face above the rim of the glass. "I have my reasons for wishing to take a wife . . . I have my reasons for wanting you."

"But why me?" she whispered, like someone lowering their voice in the dark, where some kind of menace lurked and might pounce upon her at any moment. If this was no jaded joke; then she ought to be thrilled, not terrified . . . but terror crept over her skin as she gazed across at the dark adamant face of this man who asked her to be his wife in a voice that was about as tender as a carving knife.

"When we have finished our meal and when the champagne has finally relaxed you, then I will tell you why," he said. "Your eyes tell me that you are afraid of me, but I can't think why when you have spent almost a year with a female Tartar. What are you wondering about me—ah, now you lower the cat-gold eyes so I shan't probe into them!"

His laughter was deep and richly grating . . . he seemed tawny-skinned by lamplight, the slant to his eyes intensified. Then he suddenly leaned forward and Altar felt as if she fell into his eyes, into which startled she looked again. *"Cubierto de nieve,* do eat every bit of that salmon freshly caught today. I insist!"

What did he call her . . . something to do with snow . . . while he was a man who smouldered at heart as a volcano does, capable of savage destruction in a matter of moments. She felt aware of him with her every nerve as she studied his face and knew in her heart that a streak of the very devil ran in his veins.

She ate her food mutely, for she was afraid of what he could compel her to do . . . several of the most arrogant strains ran in his blood and the proof was there in his build, in the beautiful savagery of his bones, and in his eyes. The proud Iberian . . . the lusting gold-seeker . . . the warring lairds of the Highlands . . . to make

61

this man beautiful women had been ravished, for Altar knew her history and she knew that Capitano Draco was none other than Francis Drake of England who had roamed the high seas as a corsair for Elizabeth the First, and when his men had landed on Spanish soil they had raided convents as well as wine cellars and gold vaults.

As in a trance Altar watched as smoking pheasant was placed on the table, and she saw the ruby wine catch and hold the lamplight. In her heart lay a trembling flame such as she had never felt before, and as the cognac ran flaming over the roasted bird, she had a crazy and symbolic image of herself, served up in a similar manner for the Conde to tear apart with his lean hands on which gleamed a crested gold ring. The insignia of the eagle was appropriate, for the eagle could bring down any other bird . . . though strangely enough it could not overtake the goose in full flight.

The Conde had proposed to her . . . the eagle and the goose, who must do her best to elude him . . . if she could.

CHAPTER FOUR

THEIR *café diable*, in which the brandy was set aflame in the coffee and doused with cream, was served to them at the divan. The velvet drapes were drawn closely across the door and they were left alone, silent for a while, so that the music sounded as if it were drifting across a lake.

"You enjoyed the meal?" The Conde lounged against the cushions, his long legs stretched out, his coffee cup looking small in his hand.

"Very much, thank you." Altar sipped her coffee and felt his eyes upon her, and now they had arrived at the divan she just had to wonder what his next move would be. She would have to be out of her mind to believe that he had meant his proposal of marriage.

"You permit that I smoke a cheroot?" he asked. "Some women like the aroma, but others find it a trifle too strong."

"Please go ahead, *señor*." She spoke a little too eagerly, and saw his lip curl as he took out a leather case of dark cheroots.

"What is it to be with a girl fearful of her virtue," he drawled, a mocking quirk to his eyebrow as he applied a flame to his cheroot. "What has so inhibited you—that crushing du Mont woman? Yes, she likes the male of the species, does she not? *Por Dios*, the very thought of being intimate with such a woman is enough to make me contemplate the joys of the monastery—ah, that is an old-fashioned look that you give me! What are you thinking, Altar?"

"That you are the last man I could imagine in the cassock and the cowl." Altar skimmed her eyes across his lean face, with its suggestion of great passion about the mouth. "I think your ideals are of this earth, not heaven."

He smiled slightly and emitted smoke from his nostrils. "It's strange how wise the innocent can be—so you see in me the rakehell rather than the saint. The Lancelot rather than the Galahad. The seeker of the Grail without a holy pass to enter."

"Absolutely," she said, and it had to be the wine that gave her the nerve to tell a *conde* to his face that she thought him rather wicked. "You are of the lance, not the chalice, *señor*."

"Primed with the best wine, *señorita*, you have a daring tongue. I think that the father who reared you would not like it that you are Ganymede to a woman with whom you have absolutely nothing in common. *Ay Dios*, a most insensitive woman! I believe he would be quite relieved if some man of means came along and took you out of the clutches of this woman. What do you say, Altar?

63

Would your late father approve of me as a son-in-law? I am somewhat older than you, a lot wiser in the wicked ways of the world, but I can give you the security of never having to work for any more of these soul-destroying biddies who suck all the juice out of their husbands and leave the husk to be shovelled into the ground. You wouldn't do that to me, and I shouldn't require to have my shirts ironed by you, nor my person massaged with oils and creams. Surely my proposal must have a certain appeal for you; the last-mentioned item alone would be enough for me. I can think of nothing more tedious than to have to knead the face and neck of Señora du Mont!"

"Not to mention her feet," Altar murmured, before she could stop herself.

"Really?" He looked so thoroughly disgusted that he made Altar laugh.

"Oh, this is all too fantastic," she said. "I couldn't say yes to you even if I believed you. I don't—you don't—I mean, two strangers don't talk of marriage in this way. Marriage is like dying or being born. It's one of the big things that you have to be serious about."

"I am being serious, Altar, and I quite understand your feelings. I am almost a stranger to you and out of the blue I am asking you to walk on the turbulent waters of marriage with me. I am going to explain why, but I can't promise that those waters will look any smoother, less capable of tossing you high, or drowning you. All that I can promise is that you would not have to be the so-called companion of a selfish woman."

"What would I be?" she asked, looking at him with a perplexed intentness that dilated and darkened her amber eyes, set round with dark lashes that cast quivering little shadows on the pale angles of her face. "Not a real wife, surely, but a sort of puppet bearing your name? That is what you want, isn't it? That's why you pick on a stranger? Someone unhappy in her job who might be expected to leap at any offer of escape."

His answering gaze was also intent, but there was no

perplexity, no pleading, no sensitive pain in his eyes. They were mesmeric, and without pity for her bewilderment. They looked upon what he had decided to have, without love, or the promise of even a tender affection.

The smoke of an unusual cheroot drifted about Altar, and she wanted desperately to hold back her heart that seemed as if it might beat its way out of her breast. How did she combat the fascination of this man, who not only had authority bred into his bones, but who must have found out long ago that few women could resist him? There must have been many women who had taken supper with him, who must have longed to be asked to be his wife . . . beautiful and desirable women, she felt sure of that, so how could *she* be expected to take him seriously?

Altar could only look at him with bewildered eyes, for she had never been foolish enough to suppose herself pretty, let alone seductive enough to be desired by a man who was not only a *conde,* but who had the kind of personal attraction that in this lamplit room, redolent of his smoke and the *café diable*, was enough to make her head swim.

She drew a resolute breath and was about to say a polite thank-you for the honour but under no circumstances could she consider it, when he leaned forward and laid his fingers across her lips, as if reading them before she spoke.

"I haven't yet told you my reason for my proposal," he said, "and you are about to tell me to go to the devil."

"I—I wouldn't be that impolite, *señor*." Altar gazed at him, however, with amber eyes that expressed the belief that something devilish lay in his proposal. As he had once said her eyes could betray her, and they betrayed her in this moment.

A glint came into his eyes, and it wasn't all that amused, and in the stillness that gripped both of them the music could be heard, almost mocking in its careless gaiety.

"You would be enchanted by my part of the country," said the Conde. "It has great mystery and beauty, and tourists of the lotus-eating variety are not encouraged, therefore it is quite unspoiled."

Yes, thought Altar, a place and a master to set the imagination on fire, but she wasn't going to be the kind of martyr he required for his loveless marriage. She dragged her mouth from his fingers, feeling as if she kissed them. A wild and unwanted thrill ran through her veins . . . tonight the world had surely gone mad and she and the Conde were but jesters at a harlequinade. "No, it's crazy—let me go back, please, to the dull sanity of Mrs du Mont. I know where I am with her—" With him she was all confusion, all nerves, all sorts of things she had never been before. All she wanted was to be Altar Garret, maid of all work. She hadn't dreamed when she asked for escape from Amy that with a mocking smile Fata Morgana would toss her into the hands of a mad Spaniard.

"Be still, Altar! Be quiet!" He spoke curtly, as if he saw in her eyes the wild look of something trapped. A glass clinked, brandy was poured, and the fumes of it made Altar choke as he forced her to drink the brandy. "If this is how you are when a man proposes, whatever sort of state will you be in when—my child, do stop shaking and compose yourself. There, I put a cushion behind your head and I insist that you lie back and listen calmly to me. Heavens above, I am not doing anything nasty to you. I'm not beating you, am I?"

The brandy and the music linked themselves and waltzed about in her head. Her amber eyes were hazy in her pale face that had the shape of a valentine. Her lips felt stung by the spirit and had a faintly sulky look. The clip had come loose from her hair, which snaked to her linden-green shoulder and lay there with its golden tail dipped in shadow.

"There, now you are quiet and I can talk." He stubbed his cheroot and lit another, and because it didn't seem possible that he could be in the slightest state of nerves, Altar dismissed the idea even as it drifted across her hazy mind.

He lifted his cheroot and drew upon it, and his eyes flicked across her pensive face. "Strange that I should think you would be easy to deal with," he said. "Instead you are fighting me with an entire regiment of nerves and reasons why I shouldn't have you. Well, having tried a straight charge, I am now going to appeal to your heart —oh, don't worry! I am not going to pretend that I have fallen madly in love with you, and I am certainly not going to imagine that you feel anything romantic for me. For such as you and I, Altar, it is rarely a love match— ah, you flinch. That is what you don't like, eh? Facing the fact that marriage is not always made in heaven, but sometimes has its roots in hell."

He took several harsh puffs at his cheroot and the curtained room seemed to be filling with smoke and a gathering sense of drama. Altar felt that her heart might be heard, but she made no sound. She lay exactly as he had placed her and she saw his face as through the wavering tip of a flame. She felt that she was slightly drunk. He had plied her with wine in the age-old tradition of seduction . . . but he was seducing her mind instead of her body.

He began to speak in a deep, almost moody voice. "I come of a family which in all frankness has known its scandals, but this time a very innocent human being is involved and one that I cannot disregard with a shrug of the shoulders and a generous cheque to cover this latest blot on the family escutcheon. Had I not seen the child —but I have! Yes, I have seen him and, by heaven, he's a Santigardas down to his toes and back up again to his eyes. I am a cynic in some respects, but it's strange what it does to a man to see his blood pumping in the veins of a small, unprotected, utterly dependent member of the human race. I have looked at other people's children and been amused by them, but this time—this time, Altar, I have felt my heart-cords pulled, and I can no more walk away from that small and helpless boy than I could walk away from a fox with its paw in a trap."

Trap! He spoke the word with a snap of his white teeth, and Altar's fingers clenched a cushion at the blaze that came into his blue-green eyes. He was splendid then, a black knight thrusting into a Grail that held something he wanted with all his complex heart.

"I can't take Dmitri to the castle unless I take him complete with a young mother—my wife, married, ringed, irrefutably mine! I can't give him the security of what is his unless I have a partner to play the game with me—you, Altar! You with your great eyes that look as if they had only seen angels at play—absurd, isn't it, when for months they have looked upon the antics and cruelties of a social climber. But those eyes would fool the Condesa, whose own keen sight is not what it used to be, proud, unforgiving old tyrant that she is. My sins she smiled at, but those of Gregory she would never forget or forgive. He was a saint of a boy and a man—I was the scion of the devil himself. He was the heir to everything, I was but the younger brother. He was the one who—how shall I put it so you will understand? Shall I say abdicated from his duties? I was the one who had to take his place."

The Conde paused and his unusual eyes darkened through the smoke of his cheroot, and all Altar could do, as if mesmerised, was to watch him and listen to his incredible story. The world beyond these walls had ceased to exist for her and she was alone in a kind of dream with this dark and troubled personage, who had turned to her, a stranger, in his strange dilemma.

"Thank the saints for family resemblances." A slight smile came and went across his face. "Although Gregory had grey eyes, his child has inherited the colour of mine. One glance at the boy should convince the Condesa that her reprobate grandson—myself—has ensured the continuation of the Santigardas line. Though in truth the child is the son of my brother, and my brother was born to govern the province of Las Santanas. It was unfortunate that while on a tour of Europe he should fall hopelessly in love with a young woman—a dancer in ballet—who was already the wife of a musician in Russia. A girl named Tamara, who would never have been permitted to marry into our family even if her husband agreed to a divorce. Not only is the Condesa utterly Latin in all ways, but it isn't permitted by the Church of Spain that divorce be recognized, and both Gregory and I were baptized into the high church."

Again the Conde paused in his recital, as if to allow his words to sink into Altar's mind, and into her heart. "The affair was marked for tragedy from the very beginning, but it must not continue to hurt Dmitri, not if I can prevent it, and I hope I can. When Gregory left Las Santanas, I was the only person in whom he confided. I called him every kind of a fool, as you can imagine. I said that he could install the girl as his mistress in an attractive *palacio* somewhere, and if she loved him she would be happy enough if she saw him from time to time."

The Conde flicked ash from his cheroot and his eyes held a hard, gemlike quality, both dazzling and cruel. "Gregory wouldn't listen to sense on the subject—he called me a hedonist who must now accept some of the responsibility which had been drummed into him from a boy. He walked out of Las Santanas, and I alone knew that he went somewhere with this girl, snatching her away from her husband and from the ballet. His only excuse to the Condesa was that he felt unable to cope any more with the running of things and wished to lead a life of his own. He was no longer interested in his duties, and he implied that he meant to join some enclosed order and there remain. I, who knew the real truth, was shocked that he should imply that he was going away to worship, and then it struck me that he literally meant what he said. He worshipped this girl and was going to devote himself to her, somewhere in seclusion, where no one could find them and interrupt their idyll. It seemed like an impossible dream to me—like searching for a paradise where the flowers never died and a lovely face never aged."

The Conde gave a cynical shrug and brushed ash from the lapel of his dinner jacket. "My brother would not listen to argument or reason, and his departure was a great blow to the Condesa. For me there were days and nights when I felt strongly tempted to throw off all this new weight of duty and dedication which Gregory had thrust upon me. But I understood what had impelled him —he had been tied to his plough like some golden ox who must always tread the same straight line, never veering off as others did because from a boy he had always been so good, so quiet, so seemingly proud of his position. How love must have stunned him when it came to him in the shape of this ballet girl—he had described her to me, dancing the love story of La Sylphide, slim and white-clad, with soft red hair piled to the crown of her head, her eyes the colour of misty chartreuse, her mouth like a scarlet flower. A girl with none of the polish of a young lady of high society, such as those who came to supper and balls at the castle. Neither was she a convent girl reared for the exclusive love of a young *dueno* like my brother. She was, he told me, like an exotic plant he had come upon in a forest, but it wasn't enough for Gregory to pluck her and enjoy her until her charms wilted for him. He wanted to be with her to the exclusion of everyone else, and if he couldn't marry her then he would go away with her and make for them a new life together."

The crested ring glinted on the Conde's hand as he tipped brandy into a glass and consumed it. "My brother chose the girl in place of his country, and I permitted myself to fill the place that he left vacant. I shall never fill the space that he left vacant in the Condesa's heart, but the boy might well do that, and when all is said and done, it's his due."

Altar heard all the words over again in the silence that

fell between her and the Conde. His good, dutiful, predictable brother had fallen violently in love and had cast off his chains in a wild bid for freedom and the joy of being day and night with the girl who, unfortunately, was the wife of another man. A girl he wanted beyond all that he had been born to possess and care for, who had danced into his heart never to dance out again.

The fantasy of it all had deepened and drawn closer around Altar . . . the spell of the love and the sadness had crept close to her heart. She could almost feel the lean dark fingers of the Conde lifting the latch of her heart, and she pressed back against the cushions of the divan, as if to elude the touch that was not tangible and yet could almost be felt. No, it mustn't happen! She mustn't be so fascinated by him, and by his story, that she allowed herself to be drawn into his life. A wide social chasm lay between them, across which no abiding bridges could be built. He was catching at a straw in his attempt to find a solution to his problem, and a straw could so easily be crushed, and broken.

She could only listen to him and offer her sympathy, but she would not be persuaded that a marriage could ever take place between them.

Suddenly he drew near to her on the divan and his hand came to her throat as if to find her pulse as he encircled the slim column with his warm fingers. "You look at me with your great golden eyes and you remind me of a little cat invited in out of the night to share a dish of cream, and you are unsure of the invitation, afraid to relax on your cushions in case I suddenly take you by the scruff of your neck and prove myself a false host. Poor young Altar, perhaps I should open the door and let you run away—yet if I do that, then I must hurt someone who is even younger and more unprotected than you are. I fear that the dilemmas of stolen love are always out of proportion, and there is always someone who must suffer in order that the dilemma be resolved. I don't like to torment you, so young yourself, so hungry for a little

71

kindness, so worn to a wand by the demands of that female tyrant, but Dmitri is of my blood and I must think of him first—don't you see that?"

As he spoke the Conde moved his fingers so that he clasped her by the nape, and though she tried to control the instinctive tensing of her body, and to keep the fear out of her eyes, both reactions occurred and she saw the slanting lids go narrow across his eyes.

"My dear, to hell with your fears and scruples." His face had a rather cruel beauty as he spoke. "I want you, and I'm not letting go of you. You carry innocence of heart like a shield, purity of soul like a sword, and they will protect Dmitri even more than I can. If he called you mother, who could dispute it? If I called you wife, who would dare to argue with me?"

"Your grandmother, surely?" Altar had to argue with him and not be swept away by illogical feelings of pity and passion. "She would never believe that you could ever marry me. Look at me!"

He did just that, looked at her for several silent moments, and then his hands closed over her slight shoulders and he drew her towards him. She wanted to struggle, but it would be a useless, one-sided battle and she would lose her dignity. She gazed upwards into his face and felt herself caught in a web of fascination such as she had never known before. When she was with him everyone else became like shadows. When he touched her the fear and the enchantment melted together and she couldn't tell one from the other.

"You don't fight me," he murmured.

"What would be the use? You are stronger than me, and you wouldn't care about hurting me to have your own way."

"So you think me a cruel and arrogant man, eh?" His eyes probed her face, and his fingers curved over her collarbones, made strong by hard riding of mettlesome horses. To him a woman would be no more than a mettlesome creature to be controlled, for look as she might Altar

72

couldn't see a hint of tenderness in his face.

"I'm afraid I do," she said. "It isn't in your nature to be all that kind to a woman, though I think you might be good to a child or a dog."

"What an excellent character reading," he drawled. "Is that why you refuse to marry me, because you want a man who will be kind, gentle, undemanding? A protective father-figure who will allow you to be always a little girl? I am afraid in this world, Altar, little girls have to be taught to grow up, and it is the business of men who are not their fathers to teach them."

And so saying he abruptly bent his head and laid his lips against hers. "Don't you like to be kissed, Altar?" His voice was a taunting murmur against her throat, where his lips seemed to send a trail of fire down over her skin.

"Not by a master of seduction," she gasped, and found the will and the strength to twist in his grasp so that her face was in the silk cushions and not exposed to his mericless mouth.

"You silly child, you could suffocate." He took her hair in his fist and forced her to face him, holding her like that as he now took her lips with a cruel insistence. If Altar had ever dreamed that she might be kissed with a sweet and piercing tenderness that dream was shattered in the arms of this man. Deliberately, taking his time, he taught her what it felt like to be kissed by a master. It was as if he had to chase out of her body the shadow of the silly child that still lingered there, and he did it so relentlessly that when her lips parted under his, there shot through her body an agony of feeling so intense she thought she would die of shame.

His lips taught her skin that it was alive with a thousand nerves; his lean fingers traced the slight contours of her breast and when she trembled he laughed with a soft mockery in the smooth hollow of her neck.

"Little fool," he whispered. "I could make you belong to me until you begged for a wedding ring. Oh, you think

73

not? You believe the gentleman in me would prevail, or the pride in you would never allow you to beg at any cost? My dear, that would be too sweet and trusting of you.'

He gazed down at her, still holding her against the cushions, but his eyes no longer had a smouldering quality but were diamond-hard again. "You have never known what it is to be kissed properly, eh?"

"Improperly," she flung at him, and felt that she ached from the roots of her hair to her hips, and hated the way she must look with her tousled hair and her smarting lips.

"My dear," he drawled, "did you imagine in your ineffable innocence that lovemaking was a proper thing? What kind of books do you read, for without doubt most of your knowledge of love, life and men has come from between the pages of fiction."

"Y—your sarcasm is so brilliant you must have won a diploma for it." She pushed with fierce distress at her disordered hair. "I might not be much to you, just a rag and bone to be played about with, but you don't have to add insult to injury. I can't help it if I haven't had your amount of training in the arts of the pleasure house!"

"We—ll, Miss Garret," his voice grated with an amusement edged with steel, "you have quite a cutting tongue for a girl who reacts like a little nun to the attentions of a man. Where and from whom did you pick up that kind of phrase—ah, but I think I can guess. In the privacy of her boudoir I can imagine that Señora du Mont has a colourful turn of phrase. She really isn't a nice companion for a sheltered girl like you, Altar."

"Are you suggesting that you would be a better one?" Altar gave him a defiant look, then shrank away instantly when he leaned forward, his wide shoulders looming above her, his eyes mocking her reaction.

"I can give you what every girl dreams of—a castle in which to live, lovely clothes to wear, and even my kisses —if you should want them."

74

"I don't—want them!" She wanted to believe that she meant the words; she wanted to forget what it had been like, there in his arms, brought so alive by him ... by a man who had made love to many women without ever loving a single one of them. To feel as she had, and to know that it had meant nothing to him, was a kind of inner destruction of the girl she had been. Despite life with Amy du Mont she had still had a few illusions left, but now she felt as if they had been destroyed. That idealistic love she had learned about at her father's knee was as smoke, the dregs of wine, pale raindrops falling off a flower.

"You would cling to your virtue, eh?" he drawled.

"Yes—it means as much to me as any heiress who has a chaperone even to take a ten-minute walk."

"The one jewel that Señora du Mont can never exchange for all her diamonds—ah, you'd like to fly at me with claws out, wouldn't you? I want that kind of protection for Dmitri, an unflawed, slim, quick mother, ready to scratch and bite for him. You like children, don't you?"

"I think so," she admitted, and wondered what would have happened if instead of resisting him she had let herself be swept out of her mind by his kisses. Would she now be back in his car as it drove back to the hotel, to be handed out at the swing doors with the polite indifference of a man who sought surrender from most women, but who had been testing her to see if she would be like all the others and lose her head, her virtue, and possibly her heart, there in his arms that had felt as if they would hold her until she lost all three.

"W—what has become of the child's real mother?" Altar asked him. "And where is your brother?"

"Both are dead." He spoke explicitly, but his eyes clouded and sudden lines deepened beside his mouth. "We had the news of Gregory's death about five months ago, in a climbing accident in the Alps. Papers were found on him and so he was identified as my brother—there was no mention of a girl with him, and I said nothing, thinking that perhaps the love affair had ended and they had parted. I didn't wish to distress the Condesa more than could be helped, and as you can imagine she was greatly grieved by the loss of her favourite grandson, and it would have added to her grief had I suddenly revealed that he had been living with a Russian dancer instead of living, as she thought, a life of a veritable monk. That she could accept, for she is the supreme Latin matriarch—"

There he broke off as Altar caught her breath and gave him an odd look.

"What is it?" he asked, his fingers sliding down the diaphanous material of her sleeve, through which her arm showed slim and pale.

"I—I was told that your grandmother was of a Scots clan—Mrs du Mont mentioned it."

"A man has two grandmothers," he drawled. "Madrecita was lost to me when I was a boy—I loved her greatly, as she loved me. She saw in me resemblances to her family —Gregory and I were not much alike; he took more after the Santigardas side of the family."

"I see." Altar looked into his eyes, and she couldn't help but smile a little . . . blue-green as the Highland lochs, and so startling in his Spanish face.

"You are curious about Tamara, of course." His fingers locked themselves about Altar's wrist, pressing the slight bones. "News of the girl came to me only a matter of weeks ago, via a letter from a Madame Ramaleva who had been the girl's ballet teacher, and almost a mother to her. This lady was now living in Paris, and it was to her that Tamara fled, with her baby, when Gregory was killed. She was heartbroken, inconsolable, and a week or so after fleeing to Paris she took an overdose of the sleeping pills which had been prescribed for her by Madame's doctor, and the child Dmitri became an orphan."

The Conde drew a deep sigh, and at the dark sadness in his face Altar wanted to reach out, with compassion, and stroke away his look of pain and regret that two people should die for the sake of love.

"Madame had been told everything by the girl, naturally, and this good lady would have gone on caring for Dmitri, but she is no longer a young woman and she is under the care of a doctor because she has a heart condition. Finally she wrote to me, and as it would have made the Condesa curious had I suddenly flown to Paris, the gracious Madame Ramaleva came here to Spain, bringing the child with her. I rented a house for them and they are at present living here at Costa de Vista Sol."

He held Altar's gaze and pinned her to his will. "You have seen me in the company of Madame Ramaleva, and I venture to say that the du Mont woman has implied that my mistresses range from the schoolroom to the sixties. Yes, I can see from your eyes that I hit the mark! The truth is even more staggering, for it was Madame who said to me: 'There is a girl who could have a baby and still look as if it had emerged from the blueberry bush.' And she was referring to you, Altar."

"Do I look so simple?" Altar smiled ruefully.

"It is that my plan places me in a vulnerable position and I have to choose my bride very carefully. You are too good at heart, *menina*, to ever blackmail your husband. You comprehend?"

"Utterly," said Altar, and she had a vision of the svelte and ruthless females with whom he had probably consorted in the halcyon days when he had not had responsibility thrust upon him; a wild one, incredibly attractive to women, with those eyes and that sensual mouth. "It would be annoying, *señor*, to be blackmailed for a diamond bracelet or a mink coat. Being of the simple sort I'd be content, or so you think, with being a bride of convenience to a *conde*."

He smiled with the edge of his mouth. "A lack of worldy experience has a way of making simple remarks sound like quote from a coquette. So the mouth has teeth, eh? Sharp little white ones, and you would bite me with them, eh?" He looked her over in the linden-green dress; took in her unflawed skin and the lamplit fairness of her hair. The Irish blood in Altar's veins had given her a subtle awareness of the things of the night, and the chameleon trait of becoming withdrawn, enclosed, wary of people during the daytime. She was rather like one of those rare plants that unfold at duskfall, elusive, lost in the shadows to those who had an eye only for the obvious.

She sat there and as if in defence against the eyes that studied her so frankly she caught at the cushion and hugged it against her body, which was as nervously strung as that of a moth which had drawn dangerously close to a flame.

"I won't believe that you aren't moved by what I have told you." The Conde drawled the words, but his eyes were intent upon her. "You know yourself what it's like to be a child alone in the world, at the mercy of strangers and their changeable ways. And at the mercy of other things, creeping close as shadows beyond the lamplight. If Madame Ramaleva had a sudden stroke of the heart, then once again Dmitri would be without someone to love him; someone he had grown to love and depend upon. These are facts, not fictions, Altar. You and I hold fragile as a bubble the happiness of a child; if we let it slip away, then it will burst and only regret will be left where that tiny sphere had trembled like the promise of a rainbow."

"Altar," his voice sank down into a gratingly serious tone, "death is nevermore, isn't it? Cold, final and strange, the eyes that were so alive closed against life in the final darkness. You have known death, and so have I. You cared for your father—I cared for my brother. Both are gone, but between us can't we think of Dmitri as their replacement? Don't you believe in reincarnation; the giving back of the life that has passed: the renewal of the love we thought lost? You have a young and feeling heart, which is being squeezed to death in the selfish grip of a woman who cares only about her own comforts. You could give that heart to Dmitri, for I don't ask that you give it to me. He really is a beautiful child . . . perhaps you should see him, and perhaps he will touch your heart as I can't."

His smile became whimsical. "I confess to being unused to your sort of girl, for you have that rare quality known as integrity. You and I, Altar, are at an impasse, and I think the solution may lie with Dmitri himself. You must see him . . . tomorrow!"

"I can't!" The words broke from Altar, edged by panic and a tinge of pain, for he had moved her and there was no denying it. "Tomorrow I leave with Mrs du Mont. I have to go with her—"

"You have to do no such thing!" The words cut like a sabre flashing down on an exposed limb, ruthless and fierce. "I won't permit that you leave until you have seen Dmitri!"

"Y—you can't order me to give up a job that I need," she protested. "I have very little money, hardly enough to get me back to England. I have no choice—"

"You know very well that you have a choice," he said curtly, and he towered to his feet and stood there dark and imperious in the lamplight. "You can choose between being *masseuse* for du Mont or my wife, and mother to a baby boy. You could only be an utter fool, Altar, if you choose to go on being a servant when I can make life so easy for you."

"Easy?" she echoed, and she gazed up at him with astounded eyes. "It would take every ounce of courage that I have to agree to your proposal. I should have to act a part for which nothing in my life has prepared me. I should have to tell lies and be in constant fear that I gave myself away as a fake. I look at what you offer and it frightens me almost to death. I do know that in time I shall be able to leave Mrs du Mont. I won't—no, I won't be coerced into doing what you ask of me. You could only despise me for being a wife you took under duress—

someone who lacks all the glamour and wit that you admire in women. If you offered me the post of nursery maid to Dmitri then I might take it, but I can't possibly marry you."

An ominous silence fell between them, and then she audibly gasped as he caught her by the shoulders and lifted her forcibly to her feet. "If you imagine that I am going to be opposed by a slip of a thing like you, then you are greatly mistaken." His voice and face menaced rather than romanced her. "The matter isn't settled, not by a long candle!"

Feeling the demanding grip of his hands tempted Altar to struggle against him, but still vivid in her memory were those kisses which he had used before to subdue her. Those utterly sensual, utterly soulless kisses of a man who denied that love could be as his brother had found it. Real devouring love until death; honour, scruples, everything thrown aside in order to have it, if only for a few short months. Altar was moved by the tragedy of Gregory Santigardas de Reyes and the girl Tamara, but she was desperately afraid of the man who strove to put her in the place of Tamara, as the mother of her child, who would not be accepted at the Santigardas castle because he was a love child.

So ruthless a dictum only underlined for Altar the ruthlessness in this family, and she had to fight the Conde's determination to make her the child's passport to his grandmother's heart.

What of *her* heart, beating so wildly, as she was gripped and hurt by the Conde's hands? "You're hating me?" he said, but with no apology in his eyes or his hands.

"Not really—" She shook her head. "I see your dilemma, but I don't see what good it would do to drag me into it—"

"I need a mother for the boy! I need you to allay any suspicion that might be aroused if I suddenly returned to the castle with the child and had to invent a complicated story. The Condesa wouldn't just accept my word that I

80

was the boy's father. She would want proof, documents
—none of which would be necessary if I could walk in
with a young and innocent-looking wife, carrying the infant of our secret marriage, entered into at a time when
I couldn't know that Gregory planned to go away. The
Condesa has always thought of me as a rogue and it
will come as no surprise to her that I have had to—er—
marry a young English girl, so transparently nice that
she was bound to fall into the hands of a wicked man.
I know how my grandmother reacts to this sort of situation, for she has a mind which is almost Victorian. First
she will see your innocence, and then she will see the
boy's eyes and the cleft in his chin, and assume without
further dispute that he is my son by a girl I have obviously
seduced and then married. It will touch her, I think, that
I did the honourable thing and married you."

"Thanks," said Altar, clutching at humour in order to
save herself from the deep, emotional waters of this situation. "At least I shouldn't have to pretend that we were
wildly in love—presuming that I lost my sanity and agreed
to your proposal."

He was so certain of what he wanted; it was there
in his eyes, and in the way he held her as if already she
belonged to him and could never mean what she had
said . . . that marriage to him was out of the question.
It would be like his kisses, a journey halfway to heaven,
halfway to hell, and she couldn't take it.

"Are you going to fight me to the last ditch?" he
drawled.

"If I have to," she said, her chin tilted and her eyes
braving his.

"I am ruthless, you are soft-hearted," he said. "I plan
to beat you down—with kisses or whips, it makes no odds
to me. Come, let us be off!"

It was in something of a daze that Altar left the inn
with him and walked across the courtyard in the direction of the car. She had only the fringed scarf about her
shoulders and she shivered in the night wind that blew

from the jagged crests of the mountains. She was glad to get into the car, and grateful for the fur laprobe which he took from the back seat and flung across her knees.

"Wrap yourself in that," he ordered. "Haven't you a wrap less flimsy than this one?" He briefly touched the fringes of her scarf, and the moon cast a strange moody light across his face.

"No," she said with equal brevity. She knew that he wasn't used to fighting for his own way with a woman . . . least of all one who like Altar was a humble working girl.

The drive down the mountains was fast and deliberately nerve-racking. The landscape gleamed black and white in the rays of the moon that rode like a witch above the majestic peaks. Tall evergreen trees stood sentinel at the bends in the steep road, wrapped as if in long cloaks, and the big car sped earthwards like that chariot of Pluto who also snatched for himself a reluctant bride.

Deep in fur, and in terror of the drive, Altar prayed for it to be over. She sensed with her every leaping nerve that the man beside her was enjoying cruelly the sweeping motion of the car on the dangerous curves on the winding road. His ruthless way of driving was allied to his love-making . . . it almost stopped her heart.

When they came in sight of the hotel it almost seemed a miracle, and when he slowed the car into the forecourt Altar heard the Conde laughing to himself with irony and a touch of mockery. "You fear that I offer you captivity in place of chains, you strange girl."

"In no way at all would it be a—a normal sort of marriage," she said, and looked at him with intense gravity. "I'd feel as if I were at a masquerade, wearing a mask to hide my true self. I'd be afraid all the time that I'd say something that would reveal me as an imposter. I couldn't live a lie—"

"It would be no lie," he interrupted her. "We would be well and truly married, not acting the roles of man and wife."

"Married or not, who would ever believe that a man like you ever made love to someone like me?"

"What kind of women do you imagine I make love to?" he drawled.

"The seductive kind." Her fingers clenched the laprobe. "With beauty and a knowledge of men. Anyone can see that I'm not your type—you'll never convince your grandmother that you ever felt passionate about me."

"On the contrary, Altar," he was softly laughing at her again, "my grandmother will take it for granted that your lack of sophistication acted like a spur to my curiosity—and don't be so modest about your appeal to the male of the species. You have skin like silk, the pale kind that the nuns used to make the lingerie of convent brides. And you have hair that has unskeined itself from the edge of the sun. Don't, *menina*, take it so for granted that my family will see nothing in you for a man like myself to want. Innocence can act like a magnet to the—er—sinful, shall I say? In any case, the Condesa will be so delighted to have a grandson that she will quickly forgive you for not being Spanish, and not having a huge dowry."

"I have nothing," Altar said simply. "What a bride for a *conde*, a girl with no pretensions and a mere handful of rather dowdy clothes."

"Dowdy?" He quirked an eyebrow as his gaze moved over her. "I meant to tell you how very charming I found your dress—like that of Giselle before the prince betrayed her. Is that what you are hoping for in your heart of hearts, for a Prince Charming to come along and take you from the clutches of the widow? A Spanish *conde* does not fit the bill, eh?"

"Don't be ridiculous." Altar forced her gaze from his, for he was everything—had everything, except any love for her. "Just let me go!"

"Very well, *immaculada mia*. It grows late and your eyes are like those of a child who has been allowed to stay up late to see fireworks. On the road I frightened you, eh?" He put out a hand and drew his fingers down her cheek.

"But you wouldn't whimper with your hands tied to a stake and flames under your feet. Right now you are shrinking from me with every atom of your slim being, and you are bewildered by the things I have told you, and you want to get as far away as possible—even Portugal with the du Mont seems a haven to you right now. It's an ironic situation, do you realise that? There have been women in my life who actually hoped to live with me in my castle."

"Then you have no problem, *señor*." Altar said it sedately, as if her skin and her nerves weren't tingling at their very roots from his touch. "Ask one of those to marry you, for I'm just not suited for castle life and all that pomp and circumstance. I'd be a jester at your court, and it wouldn't strike you as funny after a time."

Though she smiled, her eyes remained grave, and filled with the alarms and shocks of this incredible evening. They dwelt upon his face in the light of the forecourt lanterns, and she knew that with a thousand miles between them she would still have his every feature indelibly imposed upon her memory. Everything about him had an arresting quality, almost overpowering in its danger and its devilry. There ran strong in his veins the blood of ancestors who had taken what they wanted, regardless of screams or curses.

It was instinctive for him to reach out for what he wanted . . . she could feel him reaching out for her, and with swift panic she opened the car door beside her and leapt nimbly to safety.

"Goodnight . . ." She ran from him to the hotel doors, and the flimsy scarf blew from her shoulders, caught on a branch and clung there. She left it and wouldn't pause to disentangle it. She was too afraid . . . not only of the Conde but of herself. She didn't breathe normally until she was in through the swing doors and on her way across the lighted foyer to the lift . . . there behind the reception desk was a sleepy clerk . . . and there beyond the doors of the cocktail lounge the sound of laughter. Now she was safe and he couldn't touch her . . . but as the lift carried her upwards and away from him, her heart felt as if it stayed on the ground.

And of all the sensations she had lived through this night of nights, that was the strangest one of all.

CHAPTER FIVE

TIRED out, Altar soon fell asleep . . . only to be suddenly and painfully awakened by a hand grasping her shoulder and shaking her. The lamp at the bedside had been switched on, and there by its light was Amy du Mont, digging her pointed fingernails into Altar's slight shoulder and looking so furious that the paint on her eyes and cheeks stood out in almost a frightening way.

"You sneaking little cat!" The words struck at Altar like claws wanting to draw blood. "You crept off somewhere for hours, and for all you cared my case of jewellery could have been stolen—leaving it there on the bed, as if it were a box of candy! Where the devil have you been? Come on, I want to know!"

Altar, still sleep-dazed, gazed up at her employer without fully taking in her angry words.

"W—what?" she stammered.

"You may well pretend an air of innocence—" And in a sudden access of temper Amy swung her hand and struck Altar across the face. The blow was as shocking as it was spiteful, and as Altar's wits spun round, the realisation also struck her that Amy had returned to the suite while she had been absent from it, and instead of finding her dutifully ironing a frilly blouse had found instead an empty room and the precious jewel-case flung carelessly on the bed. Both facts would have been enough to arouse

85

Amy's ire . . . but there was something else in her manner which made Altar want to shrink as far out of her reach as possible. Amy's lips were scarlet lines drawn tight against her skin, and her eyes were hard as the stones the biblical matrons had flung at girls caught with men they had no right to be with.

Altar's heart turned over, or very nearly seemed to. She saw in her mind's eye the Conde sauntering into the lounge where Amy would still have been, hobnobbing with those other wealthy women who constantly did the rounds of the cosmopolitan sun-traps, avid for gossip and the attentions of men half their age.

"You've been with *him*, haven't you?" Amy hissed. "He gave me *this* and said would I give it to you, as you'd forgotten it when you said good night to him after your drive back from your supper together."

As she finished flicking each sharp word at Altar, the angry woman suddenly flung at her the fringed scarf which she had worn around her shoulders. Altar stared at it, bright and condemning against the white covers of the bed, not lost in the forecourt, as she had thought. Her fingers touched the scarf as if to feel its reality, and she realised with a shiver that the Conde had retrieved it, and then had deliberately shown it to Amy like a red flag waved at a bull.

Altar's fingers clenched the silk . . . that it was a roseate colour had probably put the idea into his head, and right now he would be smiling and that taunting glint would be there in his eyes. He knew women too well not to know that Amy du Mont would be furious that her humble companion had spent an entire evening in his company . . . the company she had sought and been refused.

It wasn't only the scarf that accused Altar, it was the white guilt of her face . . . white but for the lingering mark of her employer's fingers. And there in her slim throat, exposed by the pull of her pyjama jacket, pulsed a visible nerve that gave away the fast beating of her heart.

"What a sly little cat you are!" Amy swept vindictive eyes over Altar. "Creeping off to a rendezvous with a Latin rake, and coming back here to sleep the curled-up, cat-licked sleep of the innocent. If you're innocent after being with a man of his reputation, then so am I! And what did he give you in exchange for your favours— though what he can see in the likes of you is a mystery! Perhaps these hoity-toity little ways of yours caught his attention, but I'll tell you this, my girl!" Amy leaned forward, thrusting her hard, painted face at Altar. "If he's turned your head and had his way with you, then you'll be no use to me in the future. *Conde* he might be, but first and foremost he's a man, and men walk away from the dishes of cream they spill over. It's out on your ear for you, do you hear me? And you can thank your stars nothing happened to my jewellery, otherwise you'd be in a lot more hot water. Sizzling hot, my girl!"

Altar heard clearly every word that Amy almost spat in her face, and yet not a single sentence made any real sense. She couldn't believe that such a spate of nonsense was meant to be taken seriously.

She stared at Amy and heard her harsh breathing, and she knew that the accusations stemmed from sheer jealousy and fury that she, a wealthy and well-dressed widow, had been ignored in favour of her dowdy maid-of-all-work. Amy had to get her own back; she had to vent her spite, and the Conde of all people had put the fire in her eye and the whip in her hand.

It was what he had done rather than what Amy said that was so shocking for Altar. She had known that he could be cruel, but she hadn't guessed that he could be vindictive.

"Well, have you swallowed your tongue?" Amy tossed off her fur wrap and the gemmed bracelets flashed on her arms. "I suppose you were going to keep your little assignation all to yourself, but he made no secret of it, did he? What an odd taste in women he has these days! One minute he's chasing around with a woman old enough to be his mother, and the next thing you know he's romancing a working girl. These foreign notables are all a bit eccentric, that's for sure, so you'd better watch out, my girl, or you'll end up in a funny situation."

Situation? According to Amy she hadn't a situation any more!

"When would you like me to leave, Mrs du Mont?" Altar couldn't keep a slight note of irony out of her voice. "Are you giving me a moment's notice, or can I go back to sleep and leave in the morning?"

It was the first time Altar had spoken since Amy had stormed into her bedroom, and her words seemed to leave the other woman quite speechless for several seconds. Then suddenly she bent over Altar, grabbed hold of her hair and jerked her head backwards.

"I won't take any insolence from you, you little nobody! You can get out tonight! I don't need you any more, for you've done the packing and arranged about the train, and once I get to Portugal I'll soon find somebody to fill your shoes. There are dozens of girls who'd be happy to have your cushy job, and to tell the truth I've never liked you, with your milk-and-water skin and that look I've caught on your face when I've asked you to massage my feet. Making out to be so fastidious, and all the time panting for a man. It might seem like a feather in your cap to have been wined and dined by the Conde Santigardas de Reyes, but he's probably forgotten you already. Making love to girls means no more to him than a game of cards or a set of tennis." Amy gave a contemptuous laugh. "It's sport—sheer sport, and him the winner every time and never the loser."

'That's all you know,' Altar could have said, and there rushed through her mind all the petty indignities and sharp remarks she had taken from this woman in the months she had worked for her, culminating in tonight's display of envy and insult.

Altar, after all, was only human, and she could be forgiven the urge to wipe the sneer off Amy du Mont's painted face, which all the pampering with the most expensive creams could never make lovely, as the face of Madame Ramaleva was lovely.

The words were on Altar's lips, triumphant and all too true, "Tonight the Prince proposed to me," but even as she tasted the pleasure of the words, she swallowed them. No, it would go against her own sense of integrity to give this woman, with her love of scandal and gossip, the faintest inkling of that strange, troubling, all-too-impossible proposal of marriage. Even though the Conde had made trouble for her by telling Amy they had dined together, Altar couldn't retaliate. He had said that she'd burn rather than cry out, but all the same she didn't enjoy the sensation of having her hair almost pulled from her scalp.

"Please let go of me," she said to Amy, speaking almost primly so that her next words came as a shock. "Your behaviour isn't exactly that of a lady, but I suppose enough money can make a cow look like a countess even if it can't give her the manners of one."

"Y—you little toad!" Amy spluttered, letting go of Altar's hair out of sheer surprise at hearing the polite, self-effacing, long-suffering girl speak up at last. "That's nice, I must say! The sort of thing you've been bottling up, I suppose? Well, you can pack up now, and you can get out. Go to your almighty Conde and see if he has somewhere for you to sleep!"

Now in a temper herself, Altar tossed back the bed-covers and slid out of her warm bed. This entire situation had taken on the aspects of a farce, but for neither of them was there any backing down. Amy had told her to get out, and though it was way past midnight and she had nowhere to go, she would get out.

"Do you mind?" she said, with youthful dignity. "I'm going to dress and pack my things, and I promise to be gone in half an hour. I'm not going to say it's been a pleasure working for you, Mrs du Mont, and I feel sorry in advance for the next little slavey. I hope she doesn't mind cutting corns and rubbing the heels of your feet with pumice stone. I think I'll try for a job in a poodle parlour and care for dumb animals, for since my father died I haven't found much charm or compassion in any of the people I've met. They're all out for themselves and haven't any real charity in their hearts—in the truest sense of the word."

Altar stood there and she had a certain dignity even in her green pyjamas, with her feet bare. Small white feet, with straight toes and no unsightly blemishes from wearing fashionable shoes. She gazed with clear, unafraid eyes at Amy du Mont, who with a sudden shrug of her well-fleshed shoulders picked up her fur wrap and walked to the door.

"If you can afford pride, then by all means have it," she said. "But you're as poor as a church mouse and you'll soon regret losing this job with me. It's gone to your head, this evening out with the Conde, but if the truth's known he was maybe trying to make *me* jealous. It's funny, the way he brought your scarf to me there in the lounge. After all, he could have sent his valet to you, all nice and incognito."

Amy turned from the door and swept her eyes up and down Altar's slight young figure. "Yes, the more I think about his odd behaviour, the more I begin to realise that he was out to intrigue me. I mean, what would he want with the likes of you? No *savoir faire,* hardly any figure, and about as seductive as a novice. I do declare that men have the most roundabout ways of showing their interest, and I guess he's noticed that I've been preoccupied with Pearl and Sam Dawnberg. That sly dog, using you, Altar, to get under my skin!"

A trill of laughter followed these words, which for Altar just about capped everything else that Amy had said in the last half hour. In her colossal vanity the woman had actually talked herself into believing that the Conde had used Altar to make her jealous. It was beyond her comprehension that anyone with her amount of money could be undesirable to any man . . . and as she had said a while ago, first and foremost the Conde Santigardas de Reyes was a man.

"Oh, you can quit the dignity act," Amy snapped at Altar. "That devil has been playing a game of cat and mouse with you, and in the morning I'll have it out with him, and maybe cancel my trip to Portugal if he'd like that. You deserve to be fired after speaking so rudely to me, but I'll forget it this time and you can think yourself lucky."

Lucky? Altar was lost for words . . . and it even seemed crazily possible that there was a grain of truth in what Amy believed. The Conde had deliberately walked into the cocktail lounge with the scarf, and he had waved it at Amy in the manner of a matador inviting curiosity, and let it be known that he had just driven home from supper the shy companion of the widow . . . a girl with the kind of personality a man might trip over, like a kitten lurking.

The clock stirred on the bedside table and announced that it was midnight, that witching hour when impossible things seem as if they might have a touch of reality. Rich men didn't propose to poor companions, and Altar had thought from the beginning that he was playing a joke on her . . . had he invented a ballet dancer named Tamara, who had borne a son to his brother? Had it all popped out of a champagne bottle, and was this the reality . . . Amy du Mont in a cerise dress, taunting her for believing for one moment that a Conde found her . . . desirable?

Altar put a hand to her temple, where a dull little pain had started to throb. She shivered and her face was a wedge of whiteness in which only her eyes had any colour.

"Get back into bed," Amy ordered. "I don't want you sick on my hands, and you're looking right now like a cat that's been lapping sour cream."

With these words Amy departed, clapping the door shut behind her with a triumphant swing of her hand. She was of the stuff that could not be damaged as things of finer substance are so easily shattered. Altar sank down on her bed, feeling as if each nerve in her body had a barb that dug into her skin. It now seemed incredible that she had been ready to pack her bag and to fly off into the dark night. A weary, almost cynical smile travelled across her wan face. It now seemed as if Amy had the only answer that made any sense . . . her outlandish theory seemed more sane than that a Spanish nobleman should ask a working girl to be his wife.

Altar crawled back into her bed, and for quite a while she lay shaken by her outraged nerves, feeling as if she had been pulled apart by two ruthless people who didn't care a fig for her feelings.

In a while her tormented thoughts slowed down on the carousel that seemed to be revolving in her mind, and she fell as if through the darkness and finally slept . . . to awake with the rising sun, and with the amazing resilience of youth to actually feel refreshed, and resolved about her future.

Whatever Amy du Mont decided about Portugal, the one certainty was that Altar had no intention of going with her, or of remaining here at the Hotel Paloma in her employ. They had been too shockingly frank with each other for any of their remarks to be forgotten . . . Amy du Mont was not the sort of woman ever to forget a dig at her vanity, and Altar didn't want to be forgiven anything she had said last night.

The sun streamed into her room and it had a hopeful brightness about it . . . her mind was made up! She couldn't take any more of Amy's company, or her demands, and the vindictive way she had of picking people to bits like a hawk tearing at a fallen dove.

Altar laid her plans while she took her shower, then dressed, and packed her few belongings. It was still very early, but the hotel cafeteria would be open and she would have breakfast there and enquire of that friendly woman at the pay-desk if anyone was required in the kitchen to assist with the dish-washing. She would even scrub tables and floors if it would enable her to earn some money and be free of this servitude which Amy du Mont called being a companion.

Writing a note to say that she was leaving was about the only bit of enjoyable work she had done, and a smile pulled at her lips as she wrote the few words that ended almost a year's association with Mrs du Mont.

"*I am accepting your dismissal of last night,*" ran the note. "*The work is no longer congenial to me, and I am going to find another job.*"

Altar slipped the note under the door of Amy's bedroom, and then she made her way to the lift and pressed for the ground floor. When she reached the foyer it was all very quiet, for most of the guests took breakfast in their rooms. In the cafeteria coffee was already bubbling in the urn that gleamed in the sunlight, and there was an appetising aroma of freshly baked rolls, the kind that had sesame seeds on their shiny tops, and were so delicious with the salty butter and the marmalade made from the oranges that hung on the trees in Spain.

Altar stood her suitcase beside one of the tables, then she went to the counter and ordered a cup of coffee and two of the rolls with butter and marmalade. The boy who took her order gave her a rather curious look, and then remarked in broken English that she was an early customer. He was the only person serving, and Altar decided to ask him if the cafeteria needed any help in the kitchen.

"I can wash dishes." She picked up a plate to demonstrate. "Or scrub floors. The cafeteria always seems busy during the morning and the evening and I wondered—?" Altar started at the boy, and the boy stared back at her. "I'm quite good at making myself useful."

"We have a dish-washer," the boy told her. "And Marius, he is a little funny in the head, he scrub the floors."

"I see." Altar sipped her coffee. "What a pity."

"You I have seen with the big *señora*, when I bring
93

drinks to those who take the sun beside the pool," said the boy, handing Altar a plate on which two of the sesame rolls still smoked from the oven. "You her daughter, eh? Then why you clean floors and dishes?"

"Her daughter?" Altar looked aghast. "I was her maid under another title until I walked out a while ago. Cleaning floors and dishes seems like heaven compared to— oh, it was just an idea, and I shall have to try somewhere else." She watched a knob of butter melt into a warm roll, and the thought drifted across her mind that if she had not dreamed that evening at the mountainside inn, then it would have been rather nice to be nurserymaid to a baby boy. Dmitri . . . surely too unusual a name for her to have imagined it?

She bit into the roll and felt the tang of the marmalade against her palate . . . Dmitri had a charming sound, similar to the name Tamara, and she knew they were real names and not those conjured from out of a dream. She really had sat with the Conde behind closely drawn curtains, and he had talked about his brother, and his concern for the child who had been left in the care of the lady in the sable cloak. None of it had been part of Amy du Mont's fantasy; she knew that now the daylight had cleared her head, and she almost laughed as she envisioned the woman sweeping in on the Conde, primped and perfumed and ready to lay her dollar-sized heart at his well-shod feet.

She sat there lost in her thoughts as a few other customers began to drift in, and the aromas of toast, fried ham and eggs began to waft from the kitchen. The urn hissed as coffee was poured and spoons tinkled against the big china cups.

The sunlight stroked Altar's fingertips as it came in through the windows and she knew that she could no more accept on her hand the ring of gold offered by the Conde than she could wear the sunlight that could be felt but never grasped.

A short while later Altar departed the Hotel Paloma

and spent the remainder of the morning searching for work. The difficulty was her lack of the language and making herself understood in the cafés and shops where she applied. Because of her fairness of hair and skin she was immediately recognized as a foreigner and therefore a tourist, and it was either thought that she wished to buy a memento, or she wished to eat. The end result was discouraging, but not yet a cause for alarm, and at last, because her suitcase was dragging at her arm, she sat down on a bench and gazed at a great clump of scarlet geraniums and wondered just what her next step ought to be.

Perhaps she ought to go and see the local authorities, who would understand that she was looking for work, and who might know of somebody who required an English au pair. Or they might even advance the remainder of her fare back to England.

Pride, that runs before a fall, she thought tiredly, lifting her face to the sun and feeling its warmth on her skin. It lit her hair and made it shine brightly, a fair contrast to the brunette people who passed on their way to the shops and the beach. She had wandered some distance from where the tourist hotels were situated and was in the vicinity of streets where the houses were tall and narrow in varying shades of brick. The air she breathed was redolent of the well-spiced food that was being cooked inside the houses, and untainted by the scent of sun-oil and the perfume which well-off women used so liberally on their pampered bodies.

Altar realised that she was in a strange quarter, but still she didn't move from the bench, for she had fallen into the lethargy of tired muscles and vanishing hope.

For a while she had become a lotus-eater, and she sat and absorbed the sun on her bare neck and arms, for she had taken off her jacket as she grew warm from tramping about, and with her eyes half-closed and her thoughts adrift she saw odd little images floating across her mind.

Amy du Mont struggling to hook up her corsets without Altar's deft assistance, strands of brassy hair straggling against her neck as she tottered off in her absurd high heels to inform the Conde that he didn't have to be coy about his feelings . . . she had seen for herself that he admired mature women, and she was entirely his, for as long as he wished her to remain in Spain.

Altar saw his reaction in vivid detail . . . the elevation of those wicked black brows and the astounded scrutiny of his blue-green eyes as Amy gushed at him that she understood his gallant motive in suffering an evening of boredom with a silly little goose like Altar Garret . . . who was no longer working for her, but who had been given her marching orders on account of her insolence. Amy would never admit that Altar had walked out on her, and she would paint for the Conde's benefit a picture of a dowdy little virgin whose silly head had been turned by his attentions.

There on her bench in the sun Altar almost heard Amy's trill of knowing laughter, and she saw the painted fingernails lifting to the rouged mouth a chiffon handkerchief drenched in *Arpège*. Cruel, cruel man, playing a game like that on a poor creature who hadn't the wit to fall in that she was being used as a pawn!

Well, whatever his reaction to Amy, and Altar imagined that it would have been devastating, he knew by now that she had left the Hotel Paloma and was out of his reach. It had been *vaya con dios, señor*. Go with God, and I hope you find someone . . . oh, if only he had asked her to be the child's nursery maid! She could have coped with that, but not with marriage and all that it implied . . .

"What," thundered a voice above her head, "are you dreaming of?"

Altar's eyes flew open, her startled wits flew madly about like rooks disturbed by the irate owner of a field of corn. For a moment she thought that the sun had gone in, and then she saw that what enveloped her in shadow was the tall figure of a man, his shoulders wide above her seated figure, a savage flame running wild in his blue-green eyes.

She shrank from him, for he looked furious, as only a Spaniard can look.

"You needn't look at me with that expression in your eyes, as if you were absconding and I were the law with my heavy hand on your shoulder. So you planned to leave, eh, and without a word of goodbye? Was that kind?"

"I—I felt it was the sensible thing to do," she faltered. "How—why are you here?"

He gestured at his motor-car in the kerb. "Pure chance —or destiny. I was driving by when I caught sight of your fair head, and as hair of such a lightness is not seen every few yards in this country, I looked again and yes, the girl I saw daydreaming on a beach was the 'curious cat'."

He straightened to his full height and stood there with a supple ease of body, a hand thrusting into a pocket of his immaculate sports jacket. "What was so very sensible about walking out of the hotel with nowhere to go? Did you plan to spend the day and night on this bench?"

"I've been looking for a job." Altar blinked in the sun as she looked up at him, and she was struck anew by how tall and splendid he was, with a style so entirely his own. That such a man of authority should bother with her was there in her eyes for him to see, a perplexity and a pleading.

"I suppose," she went on, "you saw Mrs du Mont and she told you I no longer worked for her? Was it very funny? She said she was going to see you—"

"That madwoman heckled my man, Francisco, into letting her into my suite where I was taking breakfast, and there, to my utter astonishment, she played the role of the vamp inviting the sheik to share a tent with her." The blue-green eyes glittered with a faintly cruel amusement. "I couldn't make out what she was implying at first, and then I realised that the absurd creature had got it into her head that I had a secret crush on her and had been using you as the cheese to bait the trap. Needless to say I soon made it clear to her that I had no desire for her whatsoever, and what had been honey on her tongue turned to vitriol, and her invective was most colourful as she told me what she had done to you. However, it seemed less likely that she would dismiss you than that you would walk out on her. I made the psychological mistake of believing that if you had nowhere to go, and no one in Spain to whom you could turn, you would come to me. You keep surprising me, Altar. You are the type of female I haven't dealt with before . . . you will work for shillings but you won't accept diamonds. Aren't you being foolishly quixotic, *menina*?"

"I am just being myself," she said simply. "So that was why you told Mrs du Mont that I had dined with you? You knew that she'd be furious with me, and that with my tail alight I'd come running to your suite. I aidn't even think of doing that . . . it all seemed impossible, unreal, half a dream and half a nightmare. I packed my bag this morning and walked out in high hopes of finding some sort of employment. Now I think I shall have to go to the local authorities—"

"On the contrary, I am going to suggest that you come with me." Even as he spoke he reached for her suitcase, with her jacket folded beneath the handle. "I am on my way to visit Madame Ramaleva and the boy, and this is a fortunate chance for you to see him. I expect you are hungry and so you can take lunch with us. Come, Altar! Don't make me drag you to the car so that we make a drama for these people passing by, who will either take me for your husband or your irate lover. Though you might not believe it, Latins have a romantic streak, and it will appeal to them to think I am forcing you back home so we can mend our quarrel."

"Do you think you look more like a lover than an abductor?" Altar asked him mutinously. "Why can't you leave me alone? I—I shall be all right—"

"Don't be a little fool!" He caught her by the arm and pulled her to her feet. "If you sit here any longer some wolf will come by and start to pester you. You are coming with me, whether you want to or not." Holding Altar by the elbow he impelled her to the silvery car, inclining his head to a gawking passerby as he did so. He forcibly bundled Altar into the car, and her nerves jumped as the door clapped shut beside her; she glared sulkily as he strode round to the other side and slid in behind the wheel.

They drove past the houses with jutting upper storeys, their red-tiled roofs meeting overhead, great curtains of bougainvillaea billowing from the interiors of walled courtyards.

In a little while Altar relaxed in her seat and she could feel weakly that her desire to oppose him was lessening, being sapped by his self-assurance and his power.

"Why keep fighting me, Altar?" he murmured. "It's so much less wearing on the nerves and emotions for a woman to give in to a man. It's like the *sevillano, mia*. Relax and enjoy it and don't try to figure out each move."

"That's typical of a man," she rejoined. "You think you've only to look at a woman and she's in love with you. You've only to touch her and she's yours. Oh, I know what you're thinking as you sit there smiling!"

"And what am I thinking, *menina*?"

"That only a stupid little virgin would be in such a panic."

"I don't think you're stupid, but I do wonder about the state of panic. Most young women are only too pleased to receive a proposal of marriage."

"Most young women, *señor*, aren't proposed to by members of the Spanish aristocracy."

"So there would be none of this painful self-questioning if I were an ordinary young man who wished to be your husband?"

Altar shot a look at his imposing profile and the way the thick black hair sprang back from his brow. The bold line of his lips was emphasised by their tightness, and the cleft in his chin was centred with deadly accuracy. He would not have been an ordinary man in any circumstance; despot or dustman, he was still outstanding.

"Now it is your turn to smile," he drawled. "May I know why?"

"You would still scare me half to death if you were the chauffeur of this resplendent car instead of the owner —you just don't look like an ordinary man."

"Do I look as if I come from Mars?" he asked drily.

Her smile deepened. "You look like Mars himself."

"The Roman god of battle, eh, who smiteth down with iron those who oppose him. You make me seem very formidable."

"You are formidable, and not altogether kind. It wasn't nice of you to take my scarf to Amy du Mont—she wasn't very pleasant about it. She implied—all sorts of things."

"I can imagine." His lips quirked as he shot a look at Altar. "It was what I expected from her, but you went and did the unexpected thing, *mia*. Tell me, what kind of work did you hope to find?"

"Oh, anything within reason," she hedged. "Just for a week or two until I had enough money to pay my fare back to England. I couldn't stay with Mrs du Mont, not after the things we said to each other."

"Ah, so you retaliated? You were not going to have it implied that you had played fast and loose with a man, even though it meant trudging the streets with a suitcase in the unlikely attempt to find a more beneficent woman in need of a companion."

"I'd have scrubbed floors," Altar admitted. "But I just don't know the language and it makes it difficult trying to explain myself."

"You really would prefer to scrub floors to doing what I ask of you?" The car stood stationary at a crossing, and the Conde turned upon Altar a pair of eyes in which blue sparks seemed to fly at her. "What is the matter with you, have you a martyr complex?"

"I think if I had one of those I'd marry you," Altar rejoined. "If I did what you asked of me I'd never have another tranquil moment. I'd feel as if I were walking on quicksands that at any time could drag me down, and there'd be no one who really cared to pull me out and I'd choke on all the falseness and the lies."

"Altar, child," his hands gripped the wheel as they drove on again, "do you honestly take me for a man who would not stand firmly behind you in this undertaking? I realise more forcibly than you the perils involved, but I think I have the nerve, and you have the courage, to take them on. You look quiet, but there is a streak of venturesome spirit in you, and the kindness of someone unspoiled. And don't you think it must have been destiny that made you pause and sit on that bench just as I came driving by? If we had been meant not to meet again, then we would not have met, Altar. You would by now be on your knees scrubbing a floor, and I should be driving alone through the gates of Madame Ramaleva's house."

Altar felt the smooth motion of the car as it turned on the short driveway and came to a halt at the base of some wide stone steps. There were stone urns on pedestals that spilled petals and leaves down the stems of the pots, and as she and the Conde alighted from the car, the front door opened above them and a dark-clad manservant stood ready to usher them into the quiet, almost secluded house, with many of its windows shuttered against the sun.

They entered the cool and shadowy hall, made fragrant by the many vases of flowers that to Altar's eyes were arranged with almost a balletic grace in keeping with the gracefulness of the woman she had seen in the Conde's company, yet whom she never thought to meet in such strange circumstances.

They were shown into a *sala* whose walls were a translucent sky-blue colour. A huge panel carpet of exquisite workmanship covered the floor and the fireplace was of sheer white marble, the kind of which a hero's headstone is made. At either side of the fireplace were lovely scrolled mirrors, and against the blue walls stood cabinets of tortoiseshell, and chairs in rose and silver brocade, with matching sofas.

The Conde walked to the fireplace and stood tall and dark against the ghostly marble, where in a pair of silver vases stood single scarlet roses.

A red rose for Tamara, thought Altar. And a red rose for the man with whom she had lived, and for whom she had died.

"This is a lovely room," she said, for the silence was nerve-racking and the coolness made her shiver after the warmth of the sun. The long silvery drapes were half-pulled at the windows, keeping the sunlight at bay, and a tiny shaft struck her heart that a child should dwell in such a quiet, lovely tomb.

"Yes," said the Conde, and he laid his hand upon the white marble, and Altar stared at the contrast between the warm, living flesh and the cold pallor of what his fingers gripped. He, too, was feeling the chill and hearing the whisper of ghosts in the shadowy blue corners of the room. He had said that soon Madame Ramaleva would join the young dancer and her Latin lover in that kingdom where flesh could not feel and the heart no longer beat with the joys and terrors of love.

Altar felt her own heart beating fast, for she had never known that kind of love, and if she let herself be drawn into the Conde's web of intrigue she might never know what it felt like to be wanted for herself. He wanted her for the sake of the child, and at any moment that white door would open and she would be face to face with something that might break her resistance to threat and blandishment.

CHAPTER SIX

"I SHOULDN'T have come here!" Altar thought wildly. "If only I could get away, out of reach of these people of a world not mine, to whom I'm just a useful piece of jetsam. To them I'm not a person—I'm just someone to be turned into a wife and mother in name only!"

"You have the eyes of a creature in a trap!"

The sudden words struck at her and made her jump as if from a whiplash. Her trapped expression, the poignant appeal of her body, the way her hair swung on the exposed stem of her neck, they made no alteration in the stern look that the Conde bent upon her.

"You will at least admit that it's a silken trap," he drawled.

"It's cold." She clasped her own bare arms. "Beautiful but cold."

"Warmer for a child in those young arms of yours, Altar." His gaze slid up and down her arms. "It should appeal to you, little virgin, to have given to you a baby ready made and out of the blue. The ideal way for you to become a mother, for you look too astonishingly innocent for the real thing."

"Which would surely defeat your purpose," she fought back, a flush running under her skin and up over her neck and face at the way he regarded her. "I look what I am, and can't pretend to be what I'm not."

"You look, *menina*, as if you could be taken advantage of."

"And is that what you are doing?"

"Exactly. I have a better reason than Amy du Mont, or any other rich woman looking for a loyal and uncomplaining companion . . . and here comes Madame Ramaleva with my reason!"

The door opened as he spoke and in came the slim, elegant, still lovely woman to whom Tamara had trusted her baby son. Madame was carrying the child in a pale blue shawl, and Altar felt an almost painful lurch of the heart as the Conde strode across the room and accepted Dmitri into his own arms. There was none of the usual masculine hesitancy about the action, as if he felt that he might hurt the child or drop him. In all things he was supremely assured, and with the boy firmly cradled in the crook of his arm, he then took Madame's hand and raised it to his lips.

"I hope, *señora*, that you are feeling well today?" he said.

"All the better, Señor Conde, for seeing you." The voice matched the gracious looks. "You will be staying for lunch—both of you?" Madame Ramaleva glanced in Altar's direction, and though there was a certain kindness in her eyes, there was also a questioning look which Altar knew had nothing to do with the invitation to lunch.

"Altar, you must meet formally the good friend about whom I spoke." As the Conde made the introduction he moved towards Altar until she was looking directly into the enormous jewel-blue eyes of the child who lay so contentedly in the crook of the masculine arm, waving plump fists and kicking his feet free of the shawl. It was entirely true to say that never had Altar seen a child more attractive, the black hair glossy as silk across the well-shaped head, and at the base of the chin, exactly centred, the dimple that promised one day to be as deep as the Conde's.

"Dimple in the chin, devil within." Altar spoke the words almost unaware, and heard the Conde accept them with a soft grating laugh.

"So you see at once Dmitri's likeness to me," he said, and it was a statement, not a question.

"I'd have to be blind." Altar was deeply shaken by her

104

first glimpse of the baby boy whom the Conde claimed had been fathered by his brother. But the child was so incredibly like Estuardo Santigardas de Reyes that Altar was wildly tempted to disbelieve his story . . . and as she looked at him her suspicion was there in her eyes for him to see.

"Make no mistake, Altar," his black brows drew together in a forbidding frown above his blue-green eyes, "I have told you nothing but the truth, and Madame Ramaleva will assure you that we are not playing any tricks on you. The likeness startled me as much as it has just shocked you, but I knew nothing of this child until Madame wrote to me from Paris."

"That is true, my dear," said Madame. "You must trust us as we are trusting you. I knew the child's mother from a child herself, and when she came to me in France she was in a desperate state of unhappiness. The man she adored had been killed—that man was the Conde's brother. She had a photograph of them together in the Alps, but I destroyed it when the Señor Conde and I decided that Dmitri must become his son."

Altar glanced at the Conde and watched as he stroked a finger across the boy's hair that was as dark as his own. "This young man must grow up to claim his heritage, and it's my task to see that he does. Just look at him, Altar! Can the woman in you deny him the chance to grow up in the house to which he belongs, respected and loved and wanted *as my son*. I may not be the good man that Gregory was, nor do I make claims that I shall do a better job than he would have done, but I do care about my province and my people and they know this. I shall rear the boy to be strong, fearless, and devoted without being in any way a duty-bound slave. And I only ask of you, Altar, that you give up working for other people and share this task with me—surely a more congenial one?"

He swiftly looked at her and caught the uncertain expression in her eyes as she watched him with Dmitri.

"I need your very English presence by my side at the Castle of the Golden Towers, as the house of Santigardas is called."

"Why, señor, must it be me?" She almost whispered the words, as if already they were living a life of secrets. "Why an English wife? Wouldn't it be more convincing if you took a Spanish wife?"

"The English woman knows how to keep her mouth shut." He said it with a snap of his teeth. "No Spanish woman would accept the child of another woman as her own, but I think you might—I think you have the heart and the imagination." As if to set the seal on his words he placed Dmitri in Altar's arms, and when she felt the warm weight of the baby, and found him looking at her with that intent wonderment of the infant, she knew first of all a wild moment of protest, and then the baby smiled at her and set in the bare pink gums were two tiny teeth, like little white seeds pushing their way to the surface.

For a long time there had been few enchanting moments in Altar's life, but when Dmitri smiled at her with his sparkling eyes, showing the first of his white teeth, her heart fell out of her body into his plump hands.

"Already this one has a liking for the girls." Madame Ramaleva stood beside Altar, the grey silk of her dress rustling on her frail body. Altar sensed at once that Madame was fighting a certain exhaustion of body and nerves, and when Altar glanced at her she saw the feather-fine lines drawn around the eyes, the faint tinge of blue about the lips, and the anxiety of the Conde was brought home sharply to her. Very soon a new home must be found for Dmitri, and this time it must be a safe and secure one.

"Come, sit by my side on the sofa." Madame drew Altar to one of the rose-brocaded sofas, and it wasn't until Altar sat down, still holding Dmitri, that she realised the shakiness of her legs.

"Señor, there is still some of that fine Spanish cognac

in the decanter, if you would be so kind," said Madame. "I have the feeling that each of us would be the better for a little brandy—ah, to be a child again and content with the milk-bottle, and so unaware of the problems of life. Look at Dmitri! He is the lord of the world in the warm arms of a young woman, replete with milk and egg, and aware only of the comfort of his body. It seems a pity that he should ever have to know that his parents died so tragically—don't you agree with me, Altar. You don't mind that I address you by your first name, which is so attractive and a little Biblical? It is a name that suits you—a good and rare name, for anyone can see that you are a good girl, to be trusted with the tasks of life rather than the toys."

"You make me sound rather dull," said Altar, smiling as Dmitri grasped her fingers and forced them into his mouth so that he could gnaw them with his tiny teeth.

"*Non*," protested Madame. "You are just not the type who cares much for frivolity. A little serious, rather lonely, and somewhat lost."

"Hardly the type that a *conde* would notice, let alone—" Altar broke off, trying to speak lightly when all the time she was deeply affected by the drama of all this. Last night it had seemed part of a dream, but now the reality had caught up with her and she was actually holding the son of Tamara, breathing the fragrant powder on his fine little body, and feeling the wriggling weight of him.

"My dear child, no one has yet measured the desires of men, or plumbed the depths of them. Who is to say when and why the spark of desire was struck between a Spanish aristocrat and a young English girl? Explain nothing—just leave it to the child to explain everything. If people wonder, then smile and let them have their thoughts."

"*Chérie*," the Conde smiled with a touch of irony as he handed Madame a cut-glass bowl in which the cognac gleamed darkly gold, "I wish that Altar would smile instead of looking so tormented by all this."

"I have the feeling, *señor*, that Altar would never marry you unless she believed there was a certain element of punishment in being so profane as to become part of a union based upon a great lie. This is a subtle girl, not an obvious one. You have to allow her the consolation of scorpions and whips, and push out of sight the open wallet and the gifts of furs and jewels that might console the woman who feels with her senses instead of her soul."

Madame raised her cognac bowl to her lips and sipped a little of the golden liquid. "Did I not say to you as the music played in that courtyard that you were looking at a girl who like one of those solitary pools on a moorland is often as deep as the sea? I agreed that she was the bride for your purpose, but I warned you that she has the simplicity of fine silk, which can be slipped through a wedding ring, and can slip right out of your grasp."

Madame held the bowl of her cognac glass in the palms of her slender hands, as if she were a clairvoyant looking into a crystal ball. "I know, and so does Altar, that there is little happiness for the woman who marries a man knowing that he doesn't love her for herself. If Altar agrees to marry you, *señor*, then don't ask her to smile like a film star who had sold herself to a wealthy businessman. Accept that someone has to suffer if Dmitri is to be made secure, and Altar knows already that she is the victim, the sacrifice, being led towards an altar where blood has been spilled. Of course she is afraid of you! It's only natural! This excellent brandy might settle her nerves, but it won't drive out her fears."

Altar, with Dmitri in her arms, felt the Conde studying her. Then he spoke in a quietly stern voice: "Could you do it, Altar? Would you allow me to lead you to that altar?"

No! Her mind cried the word, but Dmitri nuzzled his warm face into her neck and blew bubbles against her skin. Oh God, she was accustomed to being hurt and had learned to take it, but a child was so innocent and so helpless, and there were those who would be so harsh towards him if they learned the real truth of his birth.

"Let me take him while you drink your brandy." The Conde lifted the boy out of her arms, and where there had been warmth there was a sudden feeling of coldness. When the cognac glass was placed in her hand the facets were hard after the softness of the baby's cheek. She drank some of the brandy and felt suddenly a little light-headed. "It's such a drastic way to solve your problem," she said, still with some fight left in her, yet aware as she faced the Conde and the child that her resolve was melting like ice in the sun. Beyond the walls of this room, this house of secrets, there was no real place for her to go. She felt rather like a vixen hunted into a corner, and fear and surrender mingled in her amber eyes as she tilted back her head and looked directly at her hunter.

"Couldn't you take a chance on the truth?" she asked. "Your grandmother might be more understanding than you believe she would be."

"I know the Condesa better than anybody," he replied. "I know how deeply and unforgivably she was hurt when Gregory ran out on the duties and responsibilities of his position. She adored my brother. He was her favoured grandson. The sunlight and the stars shone from his eyes, and then he shattered her proud illusions and her trust in him, and because she is a proud woman there can be no confronting her with the truth. She would ensure that Dmitri was not made welcome, for there is no woman crueller than a woman who finds that her idol has feet of clay. Dmitri she will accept as my son. She will never accept him as my brother's son and heir."

"And so," Altar murmured, "there is only one solution."

"Only one." A brief smile touched his lips. "And like bitter medicine if you swallow it quickly, Altar, it may not taste quite as shocking as you expect it to. Marry me! For the boy's sake—you like him, don't you?"

"He's—beautiful," she said. Then she glanced rather

wildly at Madame Ramaleva. "Must I—is there no other way?"

"I sincerely believe not, my child." Madame rested against a brocade cushion, and her fine-boned face was shadowed with the exhaustion of the heart that made it imperative that Dmitri be placed in other, stronger, more capable hands than hers. "It is said, Altar, that Julius Caesar chose his best soldiers from those who plunged head-first into the deep unknown rivers. I believe you have the courage to do that, so take the plunge, *chérie*. Leap and don't look back!"

In the silence that followed Madame's words only the baby made any sound, gabbling those little noises in which now and again a word seems to emerge. Altar glanced startled at the Conde . . . he knew, as she did, that Dmitri had just called him Pa-Pa.

The moment seemed to thrill her, and it was then that she realised there had never been any escape from Estuardo Santigardas de Reyes; from the moment she had walked into him outside the Hotel Paloma she had been caught and held as securely as a moth in a web. Now she stopped struggling and gave in. With a tiny shudder she just looked at him, and he understood.

"It will be soon," he promised, and he bent his dark head and it was the baby who received his kiss. "Within the next few days. Things must be arranged, not only swiftly but with discretion. Madame, you have a nurse-maid for the child. She doesn't suspect anything, does she?"

Madame shook her head. "She is a simple country girl, whom I hired when I came here to Spain. I could not manage entirely alone, and the girl is proficient at her work, but has no real curiosity about the situation. Already she thinks of you as the boy's father and has remarked that he is the image of you, and that is all to the good. When she is paid off, and I know that you will be generous, she will return to France to marry her young man. I speak from experience of dealing with many girls, *señor*. You may be serene, for my old heart tells me that a better future looms for the child."

Yes, for the child, thought Altar, and she smiled tremulously. This was to be one of those marriages that did not betoken bliss for the bride and groom.

"Ah, you see that, Madame!" The Conde flung out a hand in Altar's direction, a very Latin gesture, that swept her from head to foot without actually touching her. "My bride-to-be smiles a little at last! Did you see that small movement of the lips?"

"Yes, I saw it." Madame looked directly at Altar, and there was in her look a certain sympathy, and a small searching light, as if she would like to see into Altar's secret heart; as if she were wondering if there might be some emotion other than compassion in this surrender to the Conde's wishes.

The truth of Altar's heart wasn't known fully to herself, and all she could admit, even to herself, was that she was moved by the plight of the child, born of a love that had somehow been fated never to be a lasting one. His own parents could never make for him a happy home, and though Altar doubted her sanity in agreeing to this marriage with a man who didn't love her, he seemed certain that it would ensure for Dmitri a place where he could put down roots and be a part of the life his father had known as a boy.

The home that was barred to him unless the Conde Santigardas de Reyes took him there as *his* son, and took along a living mother for the boy. An English girl, legally bound and tied to him, setting the seal on his great lie.

It was decided that as Altar had nowhere to go, she must stay at the house of the blue shutters as Madame Ramaleva's guest.

After lunch she was taken upstairs to a guest-room, and alone at last she kicked off her shoes and dropped tiredly upon the big bed. Strips of sunlight played across the white walls, and she lay back against the pillows and let

111

herself drift away from thought and fear. The events of yesterday seemed a thousand light years away from this silence and transient peace. That loud and demanding voice, those awful feet . . . at least, as the Conde had said, she wouldn't have to cut his corns!

Altar was partially asleep when the bedroom door opened, and she only stirred into wakefulness when a lean hand touched her brow, brushing a strand of fair hair from her eyes. "Altar?" The bed sagged at the side as a large figure sat down beside her. "I know you aren't quite asleep, and I have something for you. Don't you want to see what it is?"

The deep, foreign, meaningful tones of his voice, and his presence there in her bedroom, seemed to vibrate through Altar in a way she had never known before. She tightened herself against such a feeling and slowly opened her eyes so that she saw him. "Y—you don't have to give me anything—" and there her voice faded away as he leaned over her and she saw the sensuous slant of his eyes, their colour darkened by the shadows that had come into the room with the approach of dusk.

"I have to give you a ring, *chiquilla nieve*, and you will take it. Your hand, if you please, and no more of those arguments of which there have been so many. Such a lot of obstinacy packed into such a slim body!" As he spoke he took hold of her left hand, and now that his touch was that of a husband-to-be it had an electrifying intimacy that struck through Altar like a shock. It made her realise that even if he didn't love her, he would have every right to make love to her, and as she lay there looking up into his dark face she remembered anew the feel of those bold lips on hers, so hard and warm, so sure of their power, so expert at the language of passion.

She dragged her gaze away from those lips that could make a wanton of any woman, and she saw the dark gleam of gems as he slipped a ring on to her finger. Stones deep red as blood and wine . . . rubies that seemed to burn against her skin, flawless and deeply scarlet as the incredible beauty of sunset over the sea. Wonderful jewels! Glowing and live with tiny fires.

Confused and deeply disturbed, Altar flicked a glance across the Conde's face, not daring to look into his eyes. So much beauty and so much value gleamed on her hand with the short fingernails. So much past history, and so much future tumult.

"It is customary for a girl to be delighted by her engagement ring," he drawled. "Don't you care for rubies? Is there some English superstition that they denote war and rapine?"

"I'm overwhelmed," she said shakily. "I never expected anything like this—the ring is too beautiful—too valuable, for someone like me."

"My extremely foolish and modest child," he carried her ringed hand to his lips and his breath was like a soft fire across her fingers, "you will have to learn not to speak in such disparaging terms of yourself in front of the Condesa. I don't want her to think I've married a scullerymaid."

"Well, it isn't far off the mark," said Altar, and shivered deep inside her body as the Conde pressed his lips to her hand. "I can't pretend to be a grand lady when all the time I'm just a plain working girl. I hope you don't expect me to put on airs and graces—oh God, what a gawk I'd look! What a clown!"

"Stop that!" he ordered, and with the barest effort he pulled her into his arms and every bit of strength seemed to go out of her as she was made helpless by him. She could only look at him and see no tenderness in his eyes only the adamantine gleam of triumph. He had what he wanted, and holding her against the pillows he bent his dark head and closed her lips with his for long breathless seconds, only to break the kiss so his mouth could travel into the soft hollow of her neck.

The feeling that shot through her as she felt his mouth against her throat was so like a pain that she actually moaned and clenched the broad shoulders that loomed

113

over her. She felt the warmth of his face pressed against her skin and she caught the murmur of some words she was too confused to understand.

"Don't!" She cried out the word and almost broke her neck as she jerked away from him. "Y—you aren't being fair—you promised—please don't!"

He stared down into her eyes, and his were smouldering behind the lowered black lashes. Then across his face there stole a taunting look. "What, I wonder, would it take to melt you into a real woman, my snow girl? Do you plan to behave like this when we are married?"

"You—you don't care for me," she said, the pain in her voice. "You only think that if you make me—want you, then I shall look more like the enslaved young wife, and be more convincing in front of your grandmother, It's unfair!"

"Really?" he drawled. "All is fair in love and war, and though it might certainly be a good idea if you looked fascinated by me instead of frightened out of your wits, I should like to know what I am supposed to have promised with regard to our—relationship?"

"You implied that you'd leave me alone—" She shrank as his fingers slid down her bare arm, brushing her skin with a deliberately sensuous movement. "You aren't doing that at all—well, it won't make me love you, but it might make me hate you!"

"Hating is for heartless people, *amiga*, and here under my hand there beats a wild young heart." His eyes held her mesmerised as he caressed her softness, brushing his fingers across her breast. "You want our marriage to be only words on a cold legal document, *mia*?"

"We don't love each other, and I won't be used—"

"That isn't a very nice word, Altar," he reproved, the glimmer of a mocking smile in his eyes as they wandered over her. The bed was a big one and she looked very slim as she lay there, held to the coverlet by his arms, her hair a tousled skein of silk across the white cambric of the pillows.

"It's explicit," she flung at him, and she could feel the hotness sweeping into her cheeks as his fingers played with the tiny pearl buttons that fastened the front of her plain and sleeveless blouse. The lids of his eyes seemed heavy and carved across the blue-green irises, and she knew he could feel the thudding of her heart as he deliberately opened three of those buttons, until he slid the thin material off her shoulder. She wouldn't panic, she told herself wildly. It was what he wanted, an uncivilized struggle that would end in her total sublimation. She conquered the urge to fight against his touch, and tried desperately to ignore the sensations invoked by the feel of his lips against the bare and vulnerable skin that no man had ever touched or kissed before he had come into her life with his fantastic proposal.

"You will need some finer clothes than these," he said, and she knew from the look in his eyes that he had sensed her thoughts and felt the tension in her body. "It won't do for the servants at the castle to see you dressed like a working girl—I can't spare you in these matters, my dear. Madame Ramaleva will have to take your measurements and an order for various outfits will have to be placed at one of the big shops. You must have a lingerie made of silk, day and evening dresses, suits and a riding-habit. You will also need shoes and other accessories—*Por Dios,* do try and look as if it will be a pleasure instead of a burden to wear attractive garments. Be a woman in that even if you can't be a woman in my arms!"

"I wish—" Altar caught her breath and sighed. "You are more of a tyrant than Amy du Mont ever was!"

"Surely you realise, Altar, that you can't arrive at the castle looking the dowdy companion?" he said, with a touch of exasperation.

"Fine feathers won't completely transform me—I'm no swan!"

"Nor are you an ugly duckling, *amiga.* More of a silly little goose."

"But one who couldn't out-fly the eagle. You got me in
115

the end, didn't you, Señor Conde?" And somehow her words were significant, for he seemed like an eagle who with ruthless talons held her there beneath him, a pulsating thing with her neck a tormented arc, the veins beating blue under the white skin.

"I think I am going to teach you to want a little more from life." And as he spoke he cradled the nape of her neck in his hand and he raised her head until her lips were but a breath away from his. "A marriage such as ours doesn't have to be a cold arrangement, Altar. Do you find me so unattractive that you actually shrink from me? We shall be sharing an apartment at the castle, for I fully intend that everyone should believe that we are passionately attached to each other. For Dmitri's sake things must look right between us, and it would be easier—ah, I think you understand me, Altar. I don't have to be explicit, do I?"

"No." The word was but a whisper against the lips that made her ache even before they took her mouth. All for Dmitri's sake that she was here at all, here in the Conde's arms, clad so flimsily with her blouse buttons opened in this wanton fashion. She closed her eyes and let her arms go stealing around his neck . . . with him it was always easier to give in than to fight, and right now there was no more fight left in her. She was faintly aware of her own surrender, her own sigh, as the hard lips and arms crushed her close, and the room darkened around them so that they seemed hardly distinguishable on the bed.

"Altar—" the deep voice had thickened in the darkness, "you kiss like a little nun and you feel as though the du Mont has fed you on carrots and water, but you go a little to my head. I think, after all, that this marriage might have some reward in it. What do you say?"

"I—I seem to have run out of answers, señor." Like a sleeper in a dream she forced her eyes to open and to focus on the darkness of him, almost a shadow except that he was too vital and real to her touch; the warmth of him went right through the thin stuff of her blouse.

After a moment she made out the quirk of his lips which the kissing had relaxed into sensuality. "You said you'd use whips or kisses to bring me down, and it looks as if I'm down."

"Your surrender would never be a willing one, would it?" His teeth glimmered in a sharp smile, and then he brushed his lips against the tiny dark mole on her temple. "You have been run to earth and you are out of breath, little vixen, in the lair of my arms. I shall leave you to regain your breath, for there's a lot to be done and only a few short days in which to make the arrangements for our marriage—ah, you quiver at the word as if at the point of a knife. *Gran cielo*, I believe you are going to prove the greatest challenge that I ever took on!"

"And what do you imagine that I am taking on?" she enquired.

"Merely a man, *mi mujer*." The glint of his eyes was strange and fascinating in the dimness. "As all cats look grey in the dark, so do all men. A beggar and a king have only a suit of clothes to separate their differences, don't you know that?"

"Really, *señor*?" A little laugh broke her gravity. "If you imagine that you would look any different dressed as a beggar, then you are certainly less vain that my previous employ—" There she broke off, with a little gasp between horror and a touch of hysterical amusement. Husband, this man, to Altar Garret? The idea was so killing it was funny—Amy du Mont would have laughed until her earrings swung like bells. "He's going to marry you, you little toad? You must be out of your tiny mind!"

"Am I going out of my mind?" Altar gasped.

"You will go out of that window if you class me with that woman of the big hats and the big mouth," he threatened. "Once and for all I am not employing you for my companion, and in the next few days you had better keep telling yourself that you are going to be married—and no more silly ideas about scrubbing jobs in the local cafés."

The Conde rose to his feet and stood a tall and powerful figure in the duskiness of the bedroom. "I will go now, Altar. I leave you to adjust to the idea that in less than a week you will be my bride—"

"Can it be managed that soon?" she asked nervously. "I'm a foreigner and there must be rules and regulations—?"

"For ordinary mortals," he drawled. "I am the Conde Santigardas and I can pull ropes if necessary." So saying he left her, and she lay very still in the silence that fell, still hearing the echo of the things he had said, and feeling on her hand the highly valuable weight of his ruby ring. Her thoughts clustered and closed in on her, until she escaped by falling asleep.

CHAPTER SEVEN

THE marriage had actually taken place, and here they were driving in through the tall gates of the castle, so towering that Altar had to crane her head in order to catch sight of the armorial crest wrought into the iron-work. She made out an eagle and a sword, with a coronet poised above them, and there was an inscription in Latin words.

"With eagle wings and the sword of might, so shall we govern," said the Conde, who was now her husband. "Do you think it an appropriate crest, or is it too sweeping?"

Altar held the boy, who was deeply asleep in her arms, his head against the soft fur collar of the coat she wore; it was leaf-green over the dress of amber-coloured chiffon in which she had been married. The ceremony now seemed like a dream, but this was all too real. They were on the long drive leading to the Castle of the Golden

Towers; she could smell the eucalyptus trees and the slight tang of moisture in the air from the lake where the castle stood.

Her heart beat fast with apprehension . . . in a manner of speaking she was coming home, but how was she ever going to think of the castle as her home, and of the Conde as her husband? He had been married to her in his imposing title, by a priest in a silk cassock, in a gracious white church on the outskirts of Costa de Vista Sol. The ceremony had been conducted before an altar fragrant with carnations and incense. There had been religious effigies in gold and silver, and a cedarwood organ embellished with silver. Everything had had a mystic quality in the azure smoke of the candles and the incense, not least of all the Conde, who had worn a dark suit and yet seemed to her clad in a fine armour through which no real emotion penetrated. He did what had to be done. The marriage was yet another duty thrust upon him, and Altar herself another link in the chain that bound him to Las Santanas and the people who lived and worked there, in the fruit and olive orchards, in the vineyards, and on the plains where the fighting bulls were bred.

When he had placed the gold ring upon her hand, she had looked into his eyes as if seeking what she already knew in her heart wasn't there; she had seen only the sculptured look of his features and the rare colour of his eyes; a nobility that made her extra nervous, brought into prominence by the black and silver-gold surroundings of the chapel.

She had had to place a gold ring on his hand, and though she knew there were inscriptions engraved into each ring she hadn't dared to ask their meaning and would not be able to read hers, for as yet she had no certain knowledge of his language. She was grateful that he spoke such fluent English, and he had told her that the Condesa was able to speak good English, which would make things a trifle easier for her.

Right now the Conde himself was deep in thought,

though now and again he broke out of his introspection to say a word to her, or to assure himself that Dmitri was all right. The journey had been a fairly long one, and though they had broken it to take lunch and later on to have tea at a lovely old country place, he had not really stopped driving the high-powered car since they had left the church as man and wife.

Altar would have liked the sound of bells, but he had warned her that bells drew people to them, and it was essential that they enter for their marriage, and leave afterwards, as unobserved as possible. How he had arranged everything so speedily was a mystery to her, and she supposed he had used his authority. His imposing title and list of names was now in the marriage register, as was her much simpler name, Altar Rowena Garret. She was irrevocably married to the Conde Santigardas de Reyes, for better or worse; for richer, for poorer; in sickness and in health, until death should part them.

What lingered of that ceremony and haunted her mind was the medieval window in the chapel, enclosed in a frame of beautifully scrolled iron and depicting an angel speared by a sword.

Eagles . . . swords . . . her wedding ring in which diamonds glowed bright as flame. Just before they entered the chapel the Conde had pinned to her dress a brooch of diamonds, set in the shape of a rose . . . the symbol of silence; the emblem of secrecy.

"Thank you," she had murmured, and all she had been able to give him was a mother-of-pearl shamrock treasured from the days with her father, set on a pin and which he had always worn in his tie. "For luck, *señor*. It's all I have to give."

"Do you really think so, Altar?" That was the closest he had come to an intimate remark on their wedding day, but with a look of intentness he had removed the jade pin from his perfect silk tie and had pinned the shamrock in its place. He was a Spaniard and therefore he was superstitious and they both knew the Celtic meaning of the shamrock and how much luck it was going to take to make this marriage seem a little more than the sham it was at heart.

When they had left the church Altar had glanced back at the white belfry rising above the smooth domes, where bells of gladness should have pealed back and forth, sending out the message that a high-born son of Spain had just been married to a woman he adored. That was how it should have been, with crowds of people to throw rose petals and cheer as he ran with his chosen bride to the beribboned car.

Their only witness had been Madame Ramaleva, elegant and a little sad in her lavender suit and sables, with a pearl and diamond osprey, a gift from the Conde, pinned to her lapel, holding a few lilies-of-the-valley from Altar's small bouquet. She and Altar had kissed goodbye . . . it had lain in Madame's eyes that she would no more come to Spain and that some time soon in Paris she would slip away from life, and perhaps be reunited with Tamara and her lover, the man who had turned his back on all that he had been heir to, to live a few short months with her.

There had been tears in Altar's eyes when Madame placed the child of that love affair in her arms. "You are now his mother," she had said. "I know that Tamara would not wish it any other way, for you have a sweetness in your face, and a loyalty and courage in your heart."

Madame had left unspoken that Altar was going to need all her courage for what lay ahead of her . . . not marriage with a man who adored her, as Gregory had adored Tamara, but life with a proud, self-willed Latin who had led very much his own life until the departure and then the death of his brother. And to keep his brother's memory intact he had accepted responsibility for his love-child, and that child would become heir to Las Santanas.

Altar felt a strange hot-coldness go sweeping through

121

her . . . what if *they* had a child, she and this man who had already intimated that he had no intention of being shut out of her bedroom!

"The boy is now awake, I see." The Conde spoke abruptly. "It must be intuition of the blood, for we are almost at the door of the castle where his father was conceived and born in the Great Chamber, as we call it, where tonight you and I will be expected to sleep. It's a tradition, so don't have one of your quiet little fits, *menina*."

"I'm having no such thing," she protested, but she couldn't look at him and kept her gaze upon the wakened face of Dmitri, who smiled up at her with eyes like jewels in his mischievous face.

"Aren't you, my dear?" A hint of amusement came into the Conde's voice. "I had better warn you that we are expected at the castle. I wired the Condesa to let her know we were on our way, and as she was rather curious when I left in order to settle matters with Madame Ramaleva, she will now believe that I left so secretively in order to fetch my wife and child. We have quite a surprise in store for her, eh?"

"I—I hope to heaven it will be a pleasant one," Altar said fervently. "It will be terrible, for both of us, if we've gone all through this and she rejects me and realises what a little fraud I am."

"But you aren't," he drawled. "You are very much my wife, and we have a certificate to prove it."

"But the dates," Altar protested. "We were married today, not at the time your brother left home—"

"Yes, I have been thinking about that. There is every chance that the Condesa will wish to see the certificate of marriage, and I have decided that we shall tell her that we married in order to make legal the birth of our son. That way it will be less complicated—"

"For you, perhaps," Altar broke in. "But it makes me— well, it implies that I'm not—"

"A good girl?" he enquired. "Be serene, Altar. The

122

Condesa will blame you for nothing and will pile it all on to my shoulders, and they are broad enough to take it. She will assume that I seduced you, and that now I am the Conde Santigardas I make legal the birth of my child. The Condesa is very Victorian in her attitudes, as I told you. It is a fact that the Victorian-minded woman blamed everything on to the male of the species. Women were never thought to have erotic impulses and so they were the victims if ever trouble came to them through a man. As Madame Ramaleva so aptly put it, *menina*, you could have a baby and still look as if it emerged from the blueberry bush."

Altar sat there, Dmitri clasped close to her, and thought over his words. They made sense even if they placed her in a rather dubious light; had he had it in mind all along to change the plot of their masquerade? He had said at the beginning that they would pretend to be secretly married . . . now he casually informed her that he intended to tell the Condesa they were married today in order to give Dmitri his name. Did he realise that they could never convince anyone that they were passionately attached?

Altar stifled a sigh . . . yes, that was the truth of it. Rather than take on the added burden of pretending to love her for herself alone, he had decided to let the Condesa know that he had married her only for the sake of the boy . . . the dark-haired child who had his eyes, and the cleft in his chin.

A little tremor ran through Altar as Dmitri raised his hand and touched the tiny indentation in her own chin. It was believable that she might have been seduced by this man and had his baby . . . it was not credible that he loved her.

"*Señor*," she still found it hard to say his name with ease and so she clung to the appellation of *señor*, which was casual enough without being so intimate as Estuardo. "Won't your grandmother think it rather strange that we gave the boy a name that has no Latin connection?"

"Ah, we shall just have to shrug that off—make a little jest of it. Say it is the name of a favourite character in a Russian novel you are fond of. I think she will be so delighted by the actuality of the boy that she won't mind if he is called Dmitri or Clarence or Amerigo."

As he spoke the Conde glanced at Alfar, and when a smile ran swiftly around the bold line of his lips she knew instantly what he was thinking. She would have to pass through the fires of curiosity, for those at the castle were bound to wonder what the Conde ever saw in her in the first place to want her in his arms . . . so closely in his arms that she had borne him a child. Her great amber eyes clung to his lips, and as she thought of them, firm, warm and demanding on hers, the earth seemed to spin.

"Don't be so perplexed," he said. "One would think from your expression that you were an awful little hag with crossed eyes. You are fair, slim, quite delightful in the dress that matches your eyes—in fact, *mia*, desirable."

Her heart shook at the word; to be desired was not to be loved, but it seemed that all she could hope for from this marriage was his possession of her slim body. He was intrigued by her; made curious by an English girl who remained as sheltered as any *señorita* reared in a convent for the delectation of a *dueno*. He would come to out of curiosity, not out of an ardent wish of his heart to make her part of him.

Casually, and yet with meaning, he had mentioned the Great Chamber in which they would sleep tonight . . . together. He would want that, because he was intrigued by her innocence; it excited his masculinity, added to which she wore his gold ring and he had spoken of exacting some reward for all that he had sacrificed, and she knew enough of life to know that men didn't have to be in love in order to enjoy sleeping with a woman.

In her mind's eye she visualised the Great Chamber, which would be dusky with elaborately carved Spanish furniture, and there at the centre of the room, upon a dais and surrounded by curtains, would be the great bed in which the brides of Santigardas were initiated into the rites of passion, and where the children of the house were conceived and later on brought into the world . . . their own almost feudal world of Las Santanas, where the air was rich with the scent of oranges in the groves and purple wine-grapes on the vines. Where the sleek bulls ran free on the plains until it was time for them to go to the arenas in Madrid and Seville, to face the lean and dangerous *espada* in his black and silver suit, in whose hands the scarlet-lined cloak and the sword were weapons of torment and death.

The shadows of trees along the drive began to turn pale and to vanish one by one; that great canopy overhead was spreading open to let in the pink and lavender sky; the scents of the lake grew stronger and Altar tightened her arms about Dmitri, as if she felt that he alone had any love to give her that would make her bold enough to face his unforgiving grandmother. His fist closed upon the soft fur that encircled her neck, and was also thick on the hem and the sleeves. It was a lovely coat, and the Conde had said : "If I smother you completely in fur, then you will resemble a squirrel. Fur around your face and your limbs is far more appealing—for you are so young, so unloved."

When he had put her into the coat he had crushed the fur with his lean hands, as if for a moment he had wanted to crush her . . . as she shivered, remembering the moment, there came a sudden dazzle of gorgeous pink light and the lake came into view, holding the sun as if it were dying there, falling through the water like an enormous meteor with golden flames around it.

Sky, earth and lake were flushed with colour. The tree-tops burned, the branches darkened, and reeds whispered at the edge of the water. Altar held her breath, and then caught it, a gulp of lime scent from the great canopied trees, a smell of wild life from the islands on the lake that like a huge silver mirror reflected the castle that stood on a prominence built back from the lake, the natural stone rising to merge with the tawny-gold walls of what was a residence instead of a home, a place of towers and cloisters and flower-hung patios.

A miraculous fresco against the mauve sky, bathed in those sunset flames, its graceful towers thrusting into the heavens ... a dream that had to be a reality, for birds didn't fly around turrets that were only made of mist and imagination. Coloured pennants didn't weave like that unless a real wind fluttered their tails. Lights didn't gleam behind windows unless people of flesh and blood lit them to welcome home the travellers.

She had thought that it might be charming, the Castle of the Golden Towers, but she hadn't reckoned that it might be enchanting, with a subtle air of the forbidden, a haunting suggestion of drama, even a hint of cruelty in those narrow windows high up in the circular walls.

There in seclusion might a captive be kept!

"We are home, Altar," said the Conde. "Does the castle thrill you, or does it chill you?"

"It takes my breath away," she admitted, and her eyes had a golden sheen as she turned to look at him. "It's very beautiful, but how shall I ever think of it as my home?"

"Because you must," he replied. "You have to stop thinking about the past and you must look only to the future. You no longer work for a woman who treated you as a servant—you are now my wife and you will have servants of your own. And why do you look like that, *mi mujer*?"

She swallowed, for her throat felt terribly dry, and her nerves felt in a turmoil. "Maids, *señor*! I hope I shall be able to manage them. Do I tell the Condesa that I worked as a companion when you—found me?"

"Yes, we tell as much of the truth as possible, only you must remember to be vague about exact dates. Dmitri is almost a year old, so we met just under two years ago while you were touring in Spain with a widow. You have forgotten the woman's name, understand? But let it be assumed that for the past year you have been living in Spain, let us say at the house which I rented for Madame Ramaleva. I have now bought it, by the way, so that if the Condesa makes a few enquiries she will find that the house is in your name—"

"Mine?" Altar gave him a surprised look. "But why—?"

"You now own a house, *menina*, and there you have been living with my son. The coast of the sun is many miles from Las Santanas, so I don't think my grandmother will be too inquisitive about the house. Sufficient for her that we are married and she has in Dmitri a certain link with the future. It hurt her badly when the news came of Gregory's death, and the boy will help to heal the wound. She imagines that Gregory was climbing in order to be alone with his reflections, but I think the truth a little more raw. It was worrying him desperately that he had Dmitri and couldn't give him his birthright, and I think he went into the Alps to try and get his thoughts into order—and when you climb you have to give all your attention to the mountains, otherwise they retaliate."

The Conde let out a harsh sigh. "The tangled web we weave—" he murmured. "I know how you feel, Altar, but have courage."

"I'll try," she said, and when she looked at the boy, who was toying with the rose brooch in the opening of her coat, she vowed that she would try very hard not to be overawed by the castle and by the woman who waited to meet her. What sort of person was the Condesa expecting? Someone very smart and pretty, who had deliberately worked her wiles in order to land a Conde for a husband?

Altar watched his profile under her lashes as he drove slowly round by the lake so she could see the front aspect of the castle, glowing in the sunset, its stonework gilded by that red-gold haze, with great lacings of leafage here and there, hiding the marks of the years; the hours of sunlight through the hot season, and the winds that blew down from the *sierra* in the wintertime.

127

In all seasons it would be a wonderful place for children, she thought, and she imagined that as boys the Santigardas brothers had delighted in the islands on the lake, and the towers of the castle, where so many games of adventure could have been played. But as they had grown to manhood the place had become a prison to them . . . she wondered why, when it had such an air of enchantment.

The Conde brought the car to a halt in the main courtyard, where the shadows of duskfall were already clustering. There was a scent of lime flowers and a rustle of leaves as a wind blew from the lake through the great archway.

"The castle is like something embroidered in a marvellous tapestry," Altar said, and when she looked at him she saw that his face was shadowed and that only his eyes gave light to his face. "Aren't you happy to be home, *señor*?" she asked him.

"There are many shades to happiness," he replied sombrely. "I wonder is it right for any man to be possessed by the past, and a place like the castle is rooted in the past. We Santigardas live our days in the shadow of what has been, keeping up the old traditions, and fighting to preserve what we have so that we can hand it on. You know what I have done in order to hand all this on to Dmitri—I have forced you to marry me—against your will."

As he spoke his eyes flicked her face and her hair, framed by the fur collar of her coat. She had removed the elegant little hat in which she had been married and it lay discarded on the back seat of the car. The wind had ruffled her hair and it lay in a soft wave about her pensive eyes.

"The castle is your home," she said. "You must love it, even if things have happened there that have hurt you. Love isn't altogether kind, is it?"

"How would you know that?" His look seemed faintly derisive, and she flushed slightly, knowing how unworldly

128

she looked even with Dmitri in her arms. "When I was a boy I used to climb the spiral stairs to the towers of the castle and I'd hide there and pretend to be a rebel on the run. I didn't want to be a *señorito*, but one of the boys who ran barefoot on the farms, and one of the best times for me was when the olives were knocked from the trees with long staves. There they would lie in great heaps on the ground, glistening and ready for the huge vats in which they'd be crushed to make oil. Everything has its purpose, has it not? And nothing comes into being unless there is some suffering—you and I, *muchacha*, must do what we can to console each other."

She knew what he meant, and she looked down at Dmitri in order to avoid the blue-green glinting eyes.

"You have the authentic look of a fond mother," the Conde drawled. "The boy has taken to you because he senses your youthfulness, and when he touches you a chord of memory stirs and your soft skin probably feels like that of his mother. See how he nuzzles you—he likes the sweet young smell of you, Altar."

When the Conde spoke like that, the very insides of Altar seemed to go molten and melting. Was he intimating that he liked her soft skin and the scent of her? Was he thinking of the night time, when he would hold her in his arms and find the consolation he spoke of? Would it be endurable to know that he came to her seeking forgetfulness instead of love? Finding in her some sort of reward for the freedoms of the cosmopolitan life which he could no longer live; his eagle wings clipped by the duties and responsibilities of the province he had now inherited in place of his brother?

In the midst of her confused thoughts the great door of the castle was flung open and a small army of servants descended on the car, while a great stream of light spilled out from the hall that seemed to run the length and breadth of the castle. The whiteness of Altar's face was revealed as she looked startled at the sudden bustle of people around her. The Conde was outlined in all his

129

dark arrogance as he stepped from the car and held out his arms for the child.

Holding Dmitri, he spoke to the servants in Spanish, and Altar caught the note of authority and she guessed that he was giving orders and instructions regarding the boy. A couple of the staff went hastening into the castle, while the others unloaded the baggage from the boot and cast curious glances at Altar as she stood there so undecisively, a slim and uncertain figure in her expensive, fur-trimmed coat.

"Come!" The word whipped at her. "Let us go indoors!"

When they entered the hall a man of important bearing came to confront the Conde. He bowed and welcomed him home, and it surprised Altar when her husband replied to him in English.

"Diego," a smile hovered about his lips, "you must meet my wife and son. Altar, this is our *major-domo*, who is absolutely indispensable to the smooth running of the castle."

"How do you do—" She didn't know what else to say, for she had never met before so dignified a man-servant, who had such a poker face that it didn't show at all that she must have come as an immense surprise to him. She felt quite certain that every one at Las Santanas had been expecting a sophisticated girl of the world, and she turned up!

"We are all very happy to see you, *señora*," he said politely, and his English was so good that she had no trouble understanding him. "I hope that you had a good journey?"

"It was a most interesting one," she said. "I—I've never been to this part of Spain before. It's very colourful, and we saw the bulls. Dmitri looked at them with very big eyes."

This time the faintest of smiles came into Diego's dark eyes, and Altar could have hugged him. Though he looked so aloof, she suspected that he was one of those extremely

130

good-hearted Spaniards, to whom the young were somehow like kittens and puppies. Thank heaven! She would
have one friend at least in this great place that echoed
to the voices and the hurrying feet of the footmen.

"How is the Condesa?" The smile was gone from the
Conde's lips. "I hope my wire didn't come as a shock
to her?"

"I think perhaps it did, *señor*." Diego glanced from his
master to the boy in his arms, seeing no doubt the striking
likeness between them. "But she is bound to be pleased—
such a fine-looking boy, if you don't mind that I say so,
señor?"

"I don't mind in the least, Diego. You think he looks
like me?"

"Anyone can see that he is your son, *señor*."

"*Mil gracias.*" The Conde shot a look at Altar, and his
eyes seemed to signal that she could almost relax. They
had yet to meet the Condesa, but they had so far convinced this *major-domo* who had obviously been with the
Santigardas family for many years, probably from his
boyhood. He would have known the Conde as a boy, and
Altar guessed that Dmitri was the living image of that
child lost long ago in the proud and powerful body of
the man who was now her husband.

Husband . . . it was such a significant word, and in
order to escape all that it implied Altar cast a quick
look around the hall, which was arcaded along each side,
where oval-shaped doors led into the various *salas* and
living rooms. At the centre of the hall, dividing it in two,
was the staircase with a double flight of stairs ornament-
ed by a gracious wrought-iron balustrade, and on immense chains hung golden chandeliers of ornate design,
set with many lights that threw patterns over the smooth
white walls, against which were hung *milaflora* tapestries,
thousands of embroidered flowers as a background for
medieval lovers and court dancers, with borders of arm-
orials, birds and small animals. The beautifully blended
colours were almost as brilliant as when they had first

been worked by the skilful hands of women whose men had gone away to fight the Moors; the days of El Cid and the golden, turbulent glory of Spain.

Ah, it was no wonder that people like the Santigardas family held on to their castles and their traditions, both courtly and cruel, and much more fascinating than the ordinary aspects of life.

Altar was now part of it all, and yet she couldn't shake off the feeling that she was really a stranger who had been allowed into the castle just to look at its baroque furniture, polished by careful hands until it had the sheen of dark silk; the engraved pewter and heavy silver plate hoarded upon a side-table whose underwork was a great carved eagle. A part of that hoard was a pair of medieval chalices decorated with shells and birds, and though Altar would have loved to touch them, she could no more believe in her permanence here than that of the petals that fell from the indoor plants to the tiles that were like blazonry themselves.

It was beyond belief that she was now the *duena* of all this, who took precedence over the woman she was soon to meet; the old Condesa with her high-nosed pride and her unforgiving nature. She had loved Gregory, but she had made such an idol of him that when he had turned his back on all this she had been unable to forgive him. In a way it was understandable, and yet Altar shrank from the confrontation, and she wanted to run from the castle when the Conde said to her that they must go and see his grandmother.

"Where shall we find her, Diego?" he asked.

"The Señora Condesa is in the flower house, *señor*. A new variety of orchid was brought to her by Señor Claudio and I believe she is concerned that it should flourish."

"I expect it's monstrously exotic." The Conde spoke drily. "They always remind me of jungle spiders—do you remember long ago when I shut myself into that suit of *conquistadore* armour and my cousin dropped that black orchid through the slot in the helmet? I thought it was a

132

spider and I've disliked orchids ever since."

"I recall the incident, *señor*." Diego's features didn't relax, but again he seemed to smile deep inside his eyes. "Señor Claudio always had a wry sense of humour."

"I paid him back, eh?" The Conde snapped his teeth on the words. "I hunted around in the towers until I found an enormous black spider and I planted it in his bed. It is one thing, Diego, to be trapped in a suit of armour with what you imagine is a monster, but quite another if you hunt it down and catch it in a jam jar."

"Indeed, *señor*. Boys will be boys." He glanced at Altar, and she didn't blame him for wondering just how much she knew about this family into which she had married. So the Conde had a cousin named Claudio and he sounded a bit of a scoundrel. Did he live here at the castle? If so, then she had yet another source of curiosity to face.

"Let us go and see the Condesa, *niña*." The Conde began to walk to the far end of the hall, towards an archway that seemed dark with shadow. Altar felt cold as she followed her husband into those shadows that led away from the brightly lit hall, and she felt the breeze against her face as they stepped out under the stars that had appeared like streaks of white fire in the plum-blue sky. The night was so still as they crossed a patio that was fragrant with the scent of flowers, pale and abundant and open to the soft evening air after the hot sunlight. The starlight seemed to cast a silvery net over the castle, in which big-winged moths were trapped, shimmering.

Everything was hauntingly lovely and unearthly, but so did Altar feel . . . trapped.

CHAPTER EIGHT

WARMTH struck at Altar as they entered the dimly lit conservatory under a domed roof of stained glass that gave it the quiet, almost religious atmosphere of a small chapel. The lush scents of the many plants added to the effect, and Altar saw red blossoms, like chalices of flame, burning in the shadows, and others waxen white and saintly.

Perhaps she looked at the flowers because she was too scared to look at the woman who sat among them in a fan-backed chair. The flower house was filled with silence, broken suddenly by the boy in the Conde's arms. The place must have alarmed him, for with a little cry he flung his arms about the Conde's neck and clung to him.

"Hush, *chiquito*." The deep voice added more cracks to the shattered silence. "You have no need to be afraid, *hijo mio*. We bring you to meet your *abuelita*, who I am sure will love you as your *madre* and I love you."

Altar knew at once that the Conde's deeply spoken words had a double purpose; they were meant to reassure the boy and to seduce the woman who came to sit here in the flower-scented shadows, her memories drawn around her as the black lace of her shawl was drawn over the glistening silver hair that was smoothly plaited into a coronet. As she stirred, probably startled by the sound of the baby, there gleamed against her dark silk the chain of jet from which hung a pearl cross.

"Estuardo, is it you?" Her voice wasn't frail but remarkably vibrant; that of a woman of personality and tenacious character.

"It is I, *viejecita*." And he went to her with the boy,

134

and the light from a hanging lantern fell upon them and they were to the eyes of the girl who watched them like figures in a Goya painting; the grandee and his grandmother, outlined by the satiny-gold light, with the flame and ivory flowers as their background against the creamy walls and the monk-dark shadows.

It seemed to Altar that she held her breath to the point of fainting, for her legs felt oddly weak as she watched the scene, and saw the ivory fingers of the Condesa clench the lace of her silk-fringed saya. With jet-dark eyes she gazed up at the child in the Conde's arms, and the air was heavy with sweetness and drama.

"Would you like to hold your grandson?" A slight smile quirked the Conde's lips. "Yes, he is real and not a figment of the imagination—come, won't you open your arms to him? He's of an affectionate nature and likes people to like him."

"But your wire—it made no mention of a child." The Condesa seemed unable to accept the reality of Dmitri, though he clung there against the darkness of the Conde's suit, his arms tight about the man's neck, not exactly crying but making a whimpering sound. Altar wanted to go to him, but restrained herself. This was not her moment and she must not intrude on what was a small battle between these two proud people, the boy their reason for a truce; a tossing away of the weapons and the wounds because Estuardo was not the grandson who had been the light of his grandmother's eyes.

Those eyes were fixed upon the boy, who as if he felt that scrutiny and it touched his Santigardas blood turned his head away from the Conde's shoulder and looked at her. Very audibly she caught her breath, and Altar knew why. The Condesa saw the blue-green eyes that were like Estuardo's, and the tiny cleft in the boy's chin, so exactly centred. She saw the ruffled dark hair . . . the likeness there was no denying.

"We thought to give you a surprise, mia." He spoke that soft Spanish word in a different way from when he

135

used it on Altar; now it became an endearment, addressed to a relative instead of a possession. "I hope a pleasant and welcome surprise?"

"It is like you, Estuardo, to march in with all the *avasallando* in the world and announce your fatherhood —and who is that?" She abruptly flung out a gemmed hand in Altar's direction. "The boy's nursemaid?"

It was a cruel thing to say and Altar flinched as if from a whiplash. The Condesa knew who she was, for what nursemaid could afford to wear a mink-trimmed coat, the glitter of a diamond brooch where the coat opened against the amber chiffon of Altar's dress? Again she felt that desperate urge to run away from this situation before it was too late. Even in Spain an unconsummated marriage could be annulled . . . but, oh, God, what proof had she when there in his arms the Conde held a child that was supposed to be hers!

"This is Altar, *mi esposa*." The Conde spoke the words in the same clipped tones in which in the church he had made his vows to love, honour and cherish his bride. "*Menina*, do come and meet my grandmother, who is fond of her little joke, as you will learn in time. The Latin woman has a tart sense of humour, and Madrecita is only being humorous, for she can see for herself that your are the mother of my son."

"Your wife—your son!" The jetty eyes swept up and down the slender figure in the leaf-green coat with the glistening collar thrown back from the pale face that had the inverted shape of a heart. "It looks to me, Estuardo, as if a few of your sins have caught up with you. This girl is almost a child, and she is not of our country. She is Nordic, and from the look of her no doubt a virgin before you had your marauding hands on her. Come here, child! Into the light so that I might have a closer look at you!"

Altar's legs felt nerveless, but she had to obey or look a sulky child who had taken offence at what the Conde had passed off as a bit of humour. It had not been that,

136

as Altar well knew. This woman was deeply unsettled by the sight of Dmitri; she didn't know whether to be pleased or to pass on to him some of her bitterness that her favoured grandson had died while Estuardo still lived, and presumably enjoyed himself.

When Altar came into the lantern light and it revealed the pallor of her skin and the apprehension of her eyes, the tiny woman of lace and ivory, and steel in her backbone, gave a snort that was far from delicate.

"What are you?" she enquired. "*Inglesa*, from the look of that skin and the way you seem innocent though you belong to this Spaniard, and he has all the ways of his ancestors, let me assure you. There will be no *la que lleva los pantaloons* in his household, and you realise it, eh? You have learned already, for the child looks as if he might be almost a year old. Speak up, girl! How long have you been married to this man—in such secret, I might add?"

Altar met the dark and derisive eyes of this woman, and suddenly her courage seemed to surge back and she knew why it was that Estuardo took on the role of Dmitri's father; she saw in the Condesa's high-boned face a quality that the Inquisitors might have had. It was ungodly to be of a different faith, but it wasn't the work of the devil to burn out a man's eyes, or to put a woman on the rack.

The Condesa could not be moved from any standpoint that she took, and if she ever learned that Dmitri was the result of a love affair between Gregory and a married girl, she would make life unbearable for him. She was old, but while she lived the truth could not be told. From now on the lie had to be cemented with courage, and Altar took hold of hers as she might have drawn a sword from a fire.

"We were married today," she said clearly. "Estuardo wished to make everything legal and above board before he brought Dmitri home to the castle. As you are shrewd enough to see, Señora Condesa, it's his son that my hus-

137

band loves."

Brave words, and though they shook her heart, Altar stood there slim and straight and not for an instant did her eyes waver from the dark Spanish eyes of the Condesa. The kind of woman who should have been the superior of a high-walled convent. The kind who could not relent towards the passions of the flesh, and it stirred through Altar's mind that she looked at someone who long ago had been married against her will; a cold and high-bred girl probably taken from a convent to be the wife of a man she had never met . . . in the old tradition of Spain, which had somehow made it possible for Estuardo to marry almost in the same tradition.

"Is this true, what the girl says?" The Condesa flashed a look at her grandson. "Yes, I see that it is, for you are not the type for secret marriages, only for secret affairs."

"Quite," he agreed, and there was a faint twinge of irony in his voice. "I hope that you won't hold it against Dmitri that his mother and I had our honeymoon before the marriage? He's a fine boy, as you can see. A true-blooded Santigardas, who will ensure that our line goes on, beyond your time, and mine."

"He looks like you." The Condesa said it abruptly. "That's how you were as a child . . . one might think that butter and honey would melt on your rosy lips, and zephyrs fly from your eyes. Look how you grew up! Off like some satyr in search of a good time—gambling—women—I might have guessed that you would finally be caught by one of your—no, this time you were trapped by the innocent, not the infidel, and you married her, eh? For the sake of the boy? Dmitri you called him, but that is no Latin name!"

"No." The Conde allowed a smile to lift the corner of his mouth. "My wife fancied the name—you know how it is with women, they have their peccadilloes."

"Do they?" The Condesa stared at Altar as if never in *her* life had she experienced the urge to be other than

138

straight-laced and correct in all matters, including holding tight strings on her emotions. "I have heard that the English have odd notions, and looking at you, girl, I have the feeling that Estuardo must have had one, as well. *Es muy joven*," she snapped at her grandson.

"Yes, Altar is young," he agreed, "but she's adaptable and will soon learn to accept our ways." And then, without further words, the Conde lowered Dmitri into the lap of his great-grandmother, where he immediately fastened his fingers on the pearl cross that the Condesa wore. She gazed fixedly at the child, as if debating whether to accept him or not. Altar wanted to cry out to her:

"For heaven's sake give way to your feelings! He's your flesh and blood, and for his sake the Conde and I are bound together in a marriage that neither of us sought. If you deny Dmitri, then it will all have been for nothing!"

"Yes, he has the Santigardas look," murmured the Condesa, and with tentative fingers she touched the boy's chin. "What a pity—ah, if only my Gregorio had stayed to found his own family, then you, *picaro*, would not be brought here to take on everything, the by-blow of a girl I know nothing about beyond that she looks scared of her own shadow! I suppose that is how she came by you, *guapo*, eh? She was too scared to run away from the *novillo* who fathered you!"

At these words Altar cast an almost desperate look at the Conde. Was this the kind of thing she was going to have to endure? Had she left Amy du Mont only to run into the clutches of another rich and powerful woman who thought she could say what she liked about those whom she considered to be her inferiors?

"*Que barbaridad!*" The Conde bit out the words, and they were addressed to his grandmother. "Shall the girl and I go away again? Is that what you would like—for us to go and take the child with us? If we do go, it will be for good and you won't see the boy ever again, I promise that!"

"I would not wish to add one *sinrazon* to another,

and don't lose your temper with me," said the Condesa. "The trouble between you and me, Estuardo, has always been that you will do things in an irregular manner. There have been *novias* from the best families for you to choose from, but no, you have to play around and come by your son in a way that is neither dignified nor traditional."

"To hell with tradition," he said, and his voice had the smoothness of silk with a deep cutting edge. "It ruined Gregory's life, but it isn't going to do that to mine. I never have pretended to be the conventional Latin, for don't forget that I have not your totally undiluted Aragonese blood in my veins. Perhaps that is why I take a British bride instead of a Spanish one. Perhaps seeing your strictness all my life made me fear that I might land myself with someone in your image. *Santa Maria*, I'd strangle a wife if she had your cold heart!"

The Condesa and her grandson stared furiously at each other above the head of the child, and suddenly it was too much for Altar to bear, and with a quick dash across the conservatory she took Dmitri out of the old woman's lap and hugged him to her as if to protect him from these two fiery Latins who were hot steel on cold steel, producing dangerous sparks that might hurt the boy.

He was indeed alarmed and he began to cry, holding fast to Altar and wetting with his tears the fur collar of her coat. "I'm taking him out of here," she said angrily. "You two can enjoy your fight without conducting it in front of a baby. To hell, you say? I feel as if I'm there already!"

With this Altar swung on her heel and marched out of the flower house with the baby in her arms, and she didn't bother to close the door behind her. Hot air and hot tempers needed to be cooled, and Estuardo was as much to blame for that scene as the Condesa; his eyes had glinted as if he thoroughly enjoyed crossing swords with the old tyrant.

Altar was at the centre of the starlit patio, soothing the boy, when the Conde caught up with her. "He is all right?" he demanded.

"No thanks to you," she retorted. "If you and that—that arrogant old woman have to quarrel, then don't do it in front of Dmitri. He's accustomed to the graciousness of Madame Ramaleva, remember that! It disturbs him to be in the company of people who argue with razor-blades in their voices. Oh, lord, there's no love lost between you and your grandmother, is there?"

"Not much," he agreed. "She likes people who knuckle under to her, and I discovered a long time ago that I have a will of my own. It was good what you did, *mia*. You convinced her beyond a shadow of doubt that Dmitri is your baby, and now you have convinced me. You will go through hellfire for him now, eh?"

"I think I might." She had succeeded in soothing the boy and his frightened sobs had died away and his warm young face was pressed to hers. "He's hungry, *señor*, and must have his supper. Then he has to be bathed—I take it that you have ordered a nursery to be prepared for him?"

"Of course." The Conde's teeth glinted as he looked down at her. "It's a good thing that you didn't let the Condesa frighten you. Now she will respect you."

"You think so?" Altar's smile was wry. "I feel as if I've left the lair of one dragon only to find myself in the lair of another."

"You won't need to see her more than is necessary," he said, as they walked again into the castle, leaving behind them that dimly lit flower house where no doubt the Condesa sat glowering, too proud to let go of her saintly memories of Gregory; too set in her ways to let into her heart any affection for his brother who had let her know from his boyhood that he wasn't going to bow down to her every whim; that he had a mind and a heart of his own and he intended to use them.

Altar had to admit that the apartment which had been prepared for them was really sumptuous, though she didn't really study it until Dmitri had been fed with a delicious broth of lamb and carrot, obviously prepared in the kitchen by someone who knew what children liked, and then bathed in a rather old-fashioned china bowl unearthed from the attics. A young maid named Maria assisted Altar in the bathing, and though she spoke no English they managed between them to have a good if rather wet time, for Dmitri loved water and his favourite occupation was splashing it over his own head and that of the two girls. By the time he was dried, powdered and put into a clean nappy, there were puddles all over the bathroom floor, and both Altar and Maria looked as if they'd been caught in a cloudburst.

They were laughing and playing Piggy-off-to-market with Dmitri's toes, when the nursery door opened and the Conde strode in. He had changed from his dark suit into a maroon velvet jacket and pin-striped grey trousers closely tailored to his lean length of leg, and his appearance combined distinction with that relaxed ease of a man who was in his home and quite pleased about it.

The young maid immediately lost her tongue and scurried off to the bathroom to mop up the water, casting a look at the Conde which combined a certain admiration with a look of awe, for a quick glance at him soon informed Altar that he was looking as attractively well-groomed as she was looking tousled, damp and shiny-nosed.

"Ah, I see that a lot of the old things have been brought down from the attics and put to use. This little carved bed is many years old and will still be practicable when Dmitri is grown up and ready to start a family of his own." The lean dark fingers traced the birds and acorns and foxes' heads carved around the frame of the small bed, which had been covered by a blue blanket and a white lace coverlet, the sides of the bed high enough so that a child couldn't tumble out of it.

"This little bed was sent from Scotland when my mother was due to be born here in Spain. It was among the things left to me when Madrecita died—you would

142

have liked her very much, Altar. She had a warm and impulsive heart, and with due respect to the Condesa I remember as a boy of sixteen, when I lost Madrecita, dashing to the chapel and crying out to the Madonna there that it was unfair to take my lovely *mia prima* when there were others—" He broke off and shrugged his wide shoulders. "Alas, I was always a bad boy who did all the wrong things, and little does the Condesa know that all being well this young man will grow up to be like his father."

The Conde lifted Dmitri into his arms as he spoke and carried him to the little carved bed, where with the naturalness of the Spaniard when it came to children he tucked him into his covers. "He doesn't need a night garment," he said. "In this let him be like me, for I could never endure to have anything on me at night. Let his limbs kick and stretch in their natural state—you agree?"

"If that's what you wish," said Altar, fussing a little with her untidy hair and hoping he would accept her rise in colour as part of her exertions. He spoke so casually about the way he slept in bed, but she couldn't be as casual as he about that aspect of their relationship. The very thought of seeing that lean and splendid body in a state of nudity was enough to destroy her composure, and now, with Dmitri settled, kissed and already off to dreamland, she had to walk into the adjoining bedroom and feel the Conde strolling at her heels.

"And what do you think of this room?" he asked.

She looked around and just had to be flippant or be overwhelmed by the entire situation. "Is it the Great Chamber, *señor*? What a relief, when I was expecting Inquisitorial furniture and a bed draped in brown velvet curtains."

His lips quirked as he surveyed her, there at the centre of the soft white astrakhan carpet covering the floor, with an elegant baroque bed a little way behind her, its counterpane of lace over silk falling in graceful folds to the carpet. The pale netting was swathed around the slim posts, like the veil of a bride waiting to be lowered.

"I told Diego in a separate wire not to prepare the great old room for us, for I knew that you were in too nervous a state ever to be got over the threshold of it. Besides, we are not thought of as the conventional bride and groom. We have a son, so everyone believes, and the Great Chamber is for the virgin brides of the Santigardas men. If I took you there, the Condesa might start to wonder why."

"So you were having me on," she said, and walked to the dressing-table, which had a mirror shaped like a shield, and a white marble top lighted by small silver lamps and filled with pretty pots and long-necked bottles. To one side of the dressing-table was a full-length mirror surmounted by a filigreed coronet of silver, and the pan-elling of the room was gardenia-white with touches of amber gold. One panel of the wall was filled by a vivid painting of a handsome courtier of about the fifteenth century holding on his wrist—like a beautiful bird—the hand of a woman dressed in a high-crowned hat and a dress of rich silk and velvet.

Altar gazed at the painting, and then took a look at herself in the mirror. "I do look a mess," she said. "It's a good thing you Spanish people have dinner so late in the evening, for it will give me a chance to take a shower and make myself a bit more presentable."

"You can have your dinner up here if you wish," he said, tinkering with a little porcelain box on tiny gold feet, painted with miniature court figures. "It has been a long day for you, and I believe if you had to face the Condesa again tonight, you would shatter as this little box would if I threw it on the table-top."

"Y—you mean that—that I may have my meal up here in the bedroom?" She turned to look at him with eyes that couldn't quite believe in his sincerity.

"Surely you know by now that if I say a thing I mean it?" He took her by the shoulders and drew her to within an inch or two of his hard body in the velvet jacket.

"I shall brave the dragon all alone, just for your sake, *menina*. Are you not grateful to me?"

"Of course—I am feeling a bit weary—"

"Not too weary, I hope." His eyes looked down into hers and a faint gleam of mockery stole into them. "I shall send up wine with your tray and that will liven you up."

"Wine usually makes me feel sleepy," she said, and there was no way in the world of controlling the flush that stung her cheeks with all the pinkness of the carnations that glowed in a vase on a nearby table.

"Does it, *chiquita*?" He ran a finger down her hot cheek. "Then let me warn you that if you are sleeping when I come to bed, I shall not hesitate to wake you up. This is our wedding night, when all is said and done, and even if we are not in the Great Chamber I still intend to placate whatever gods guard the Santigardas honour by taking unto me the virgin that a Santigardas always marries. Do you believe in legends, Altar? There is an old one attached to this family, which says that if a Santigardas male should ever attach himself to a woman who has no virtue, then the vines will wither, the fields will turn to stone, and the olives will run dry. It may be only a superstition, but I believe my brother had faith in it, and that was why he went so far away with the girl he loved —for that girl was not a virgin."

"Is it so terrible for a Spaniard to—to marry a woman who has already had a lover?" Altar could feel his touch to her very bones and because she was so intensely aware of him she somehow had to fight him. "How can you be so inflexible when you have had such a good time yourself? It's the Victorian double standard that was so prevalent in England, that men may sow their wild oats, but lord help the woman who does!"

"A certain type of woman has always sown her wild oats," he said crisply. "And very few Spaniards would take the innocence of a good girl."

"But you are presumed to have taken mine," Altar

145

reminded him. "And I have to grin and bear what people think of me."

"We know the real truth, Altar." He gripped her chin and forced her to look directly into his eyes, which still had that infuriating little glint in them. "So long as I know the kind of girl you are, then to the devil with other people. In any case, you are English, and Latins are only extremely cruel to their own people. I have always had a rakish reputation and all real blame will be lodged with me—*mia*, is it so very painful to be thought a little naughty?"

"I'm not sure," she said, and she could feel little tremors running over her skin as his fingers wandered to her neck in the opening of the wrap-around into which she had changed before starting to give Dmitri his bath.

"Sweet young Altar, the bride of naughty Estuardo Santigardas." And so saying he deliberately untied the wrap-around and peeled it from her body like a skin. He then took her slim, lightly-clad body into his arms and lowered his face into her neck.

"You smell of baby powder and soapy water," he murmured. "*Santo Dios,* if it wasn't for the Condesa and the protocol of dining with her tonight, I would stay here and woo you until you stopped shaking like a little aspen tree. Does it strike such terror into your heart, the thought of giving yourself to me?"

It did, and she could only shake against his velvet jacket and wish to heaven that she wasn't such a little fool. It wasn't enough to know the facts of life . . . this man who was her husband was a man of the world, landed with a trembling virgin to whom his power and his personality at moments like this were petrifying.

"You know what you need," he said. "A monkey's tail."

"A—a what?" Her fingers clenched the maroon velvet as his fingers slid down her spine to her waist, playing with her, half mockingly she knew, because he found himself not with a woman who knew how to respond to

146

a man's passion but with a girl who, as Amy du Mont had correctly guessed, had never even had a boy-friend!

—"A *cola de mona*. It's made from Aguardiente, coffee, sugar, cinnamon and egg-yolk, and is good at settling the nerves. I will tell Diego to send one up for you, for you have had an unsettling day, have you not?" He caught at her hand as he spoke and studied the beautifully chased ring with its setting of small perfect diamonds, and the gesture seemed to Altar to signify a certain regret that she lacked the fire he was used to arousing in the women he had known in colourful Spanish cities, in Paris, Rome and on the Côte d'Azur. The cosmopolitan world had been his playground, and when she dared to look at him it seemed to Altar that he looked sombre and cynical, as if he expected his marriage to be one of inconvenience if she continued to be so nervous of his touch.

"I'm sorry to be such a wet blanket, *señor*." She shivered as he touched the tendrils of damp hair that clung to her neck.

"Yes, you are wet, *mia*. We must arrange to have a baby bath sent here for the boy, for that bowl is too shallow and he has well splashed you. Get to your own bath, *menina*, and when the monkey's tail arrives you will drink every drop, do you hear me?"

"Yes, *señor*," she said meekly.

"And that is another thing!" He spoke with a whipsting in his voice. "My name is Estuardo and you had better use it. The Condesa is going to think it strange if you address the father of your child in that formal way, for though you might look as if you could have an immaculate conception, I don't look very saintly. In the eyes of everyone at Las Santanas we have a baby, and that means that I have been your lover and continue to be your lover, and you just can't speak to me as if I were your employer. *Comprendo*?"

She nodded, and then said with a little rush: "I'm sure everyone is thinking me an odd sort of wife for a *conde*! How Amy du Mont would laugh if she could see me here, trying to look the lady! She always said that I was more suited to a nunnery than the sun spots of Europe!"

"You had better forget the nunnery, and the du Mont woman," he said crisply. "That wasn't a vow of chastity which you took today, so bear that in mind. I don't expect you to start behaving like a flamenco dancer, flashing your eyes and your heels around, but it would be nice to have a wife with a little warmth in her instead of one who turns pale as a statue when I come into the bedroom."

He had a way with certain words of snapping his teeth on them, so that their significance was increased tenfold. Altar noticed a door at the far end of the white bedroom, and when she glanced at it, he gave a mocking little laugh.

"My dressing room," he said, "supplied with a couch on which I don't intend to sleep. There is a perfectly good-sized bed in this room and I intend to share it with you, *comprendo*?"

"Yes," she muttered. "And there's no need to keep asking me if I comprehend your every word as if I'm a child—"

"You are behaving like a child," he drawled, and he deliberately pushed the strap of her slip from her left shoulder and buried his warm lips in the soft hollow of her flesh. "It's for me to teach you that you are not a child but a young woman, but right now I haven't the time. I have to dine with the Condesa and conciliate her for your absence. I am not quite so cruel, *chiquita*, that I would subject you to any more of her taunts tonight. She will be that way for a while. She is still rather bitter about the loss of Gregory and I can never fill his shoes as far as she is concerned, and some of that bitterness will be carried over to my wife—"

"But it seems so unfair—"

"That she should treat you so unkindly?" He shrugged. "I am sorry about that, but she is proud, old, unhappy,

148

and time will soften her towards you, especially when she begins to love the boy, and that will be inevitable—"

"No," said Altar, "it's unfair that she should treat you like Cain when you're really more loyal, more self-sacrificing than your brother was. I—I felt like telling her—"

"You will never do that," he said curtly. "I should be intolerably angry if you ever breathed a word about Tamara and that liaison Gregory had with her. Let his memory remain a good one, and let him and the girl rest in peace. They have paid, heaven knows, a terrible price for the love they snatched together, and it's a small price for me to pay, to take on the rearing of his child and to give him my name—"

"In taking on those, you have had to take me on," Altar broke in, a hint of weary tears in her voice. "Quite soon you're going to hate me for being part of the package, for I can't be beautiful and sparkling and full of sex appeal. I'm just *me*."

"So you are." He tipped back her head and stared down into her drowned eyes, wet amber pools, forlorn and accusing at the same time. "A girl from out of nowhere who suited my purpose—do you hate me, I wonder?"

And with these words he let go of her and strode to the door that led on to the gallery. "*Hasta la vista, cara.* I will give your regards to Madrecita, and I do beg of you that if you have to weep, then do it under the shower and not in front of the maid who brings your dinner tray."

The door closed decisively behind him, but still the room was haunted by his presence and by his remarks. That final remark had stilled her tears and they glittered in her eyes as if trapped in amber. She didn't hate him and never could, not from that first moment of looking into those eyes whose rare Celadon blue had been passed on to Dmitri through the strange processes of heredity. Seeing those eyes in the boy, and then seeing her, so obviously unhappy with Amy du Mont, had given him the idea for this marriage.

Had it seemed to him that in her gratitude, her escape

149

from other domineering women, she would be only too eager to please him, sensually?

She sank down on the bed and buried her face in her hands. It was more painful than she had realised that it would be, to find herself the wife of a man who didn't love her but intended to exact from her the total surrender of her body. She knew she could never respond to him under those terms, and she dreaded the night that lay ahead of her. She knew that when he found her frigid with terror he would despise her . . . as the Condesa already despised her.

Because she couldn't give herself he would have to take her . . . and with a sudden terrified little gasp, as if already she visualised the scene, Altar ran to the door that separated their rooms and examined the lock. There was no key on her side, but when she opened the door she found that it was inserted in the lock on his side. She removed it and went and tried it in the other door, the one that opened to reveal the softly lit gallery, where in balcony recesses above the hall stood pots of indoor geraniums, fuchsias and orange-plants. She could smell them as she stood there and felt the key turn back and forth in the lock. They reminded her of the scent of flowers in the chapel, during that ceremony which had bound her to a man whose vows of love had been profane.

He didn't care that she had a heart to win, or break, he only wanted some sort of reward, as he had called it, for marrying her.

She returned to the bed and pushed the key under one of the pillows. There it would stay until the maid had brought her dinner tray . . . no, she had better have her dinner, and then lock both doors after the maid had taken the tray downstairs.

When Estuardo came upstairs he would find the doors locked, and he would know that she couldn't go through with this marriage. He would have to let her go . . . he couldn't be cruel enough to keep her at the castle against her will.

After all, she had done all that was necessary. She had shown herself to the Condesa and proved that the boy had a legal mother. She had made it possible for Dmitri to be accepted here . . . this was his home, this was where he belonged, because he was loved.

She was not loved . . . she did not belong at the Castle of the Golden Towers.

CHAPTER NINE

She must have been drifting in that half-land between awareness and sleep when the rattle of the door awakened her. She sat up sharply, pulling the covers around her, crouching there against the pillows in the dimness of the room, lit by a single gold-shaded lamp on the bed-table.

It was late and her dinner tray had long been taken away, so Altar knew who it was who tried the door and found it locked. Her heart beat so frenziedly that it seemed to shake her body, and now that she had locked him out of her room and she could visualise him standing there tall and grim-faced at the other side of the door, the moment was actually more terrifying than if she had submitted to him.

He might be cultured and travelled, but he was still an ultra-Spaniard at heart, and deep in that temperament there was a certain cruelty and savagery; a bred-in-the-bone inflexibility when it came to women. Even as they kissed a woman's hand, there smouldered in their eyes a warning that women were meant to be conquered.

Altar breathed quickly, like a creature caught in a trap, as her eyes fixed themselves upon the door at the far end of the room . . . and then she nearly jumped out of her skin as the door nearer to the bed was suddenly tried, making a slight jarring sound that to her nervous ears sounded like a drum being struck. "Go away!" she begged silently. "Please . . . please go away!"

As if her fear and her appeal had reached to him, he let go the handle and everything was quiet again. She strained her ears, but all she could hear was the ticking of the clock and the rustle of vines beyond the windows.

In a little while she dared to breathe almost normally . . . he wouldn't force the door and make such a racket that the entire household would hear him. He was far too proud for that, and with a painful little sigh Altar let her head droop against the pillows. When she had come to Spain with Amy du Mont she had never dreamed that she would come to this . . . fighting a battle of wills with a man about whom Amy had said: "With his amount of experience he'll have no trouble managing a virginal bride—he's so immensely attractive that she'll probably fall for him the first time they're together."

When she and Amy had discussed him that first night in the hotel dining-room, it had not seemed remotely possible that Altar would find herself in the position she had decried as being like the slave market. When they had seen him at the Falla concert, and she had listened so raptly to the Ritual Fire Dance, there had been nothing to warn her that he had decided then and there to marry her.

She pressed into the pillows and drew the coverlets over her as if to hide from her own thoughts. "Why did you marry him?" they cried out. "He didn't hold a gun to your head . . . you went through with it, and he has every right to expect you to behave like a wife rather than a shivering little vixen, hiding in her lair, hoping not to be found and dragged out of it."

In a way it didn't surprise her, though it very nearly stopped her heart, when a key rattled in the lock of the adjoining door and it opened to let him into her room. She knew instantly that during that interval of silence he had gone to Diego and requested the master-key. It wouldn't concern him that Diego, whom he knew so well, would guess that he was having trouble with his bride. The *major-domo* had been with the family too long to discuss any of the secrets that fell into his keeping. He was of the type who was loyal from choice, not bribery or fear.

Altar's own fear was now at the edge of desperation, so that when the bedcovers were pulled away from her, she was ready to scratch and bite and make such a hellion of herself that he'd have one hell of a wedding night.

He reached down and dragged her up against him by a handful of her pyjama jacket, and in the silence broken by their combined quick breathing, and in the light that was filtered golden and dusky through the lampshade, they fought each other. He wore no jacket, only dark silk pyjama trousers, and when her teeth stabbed at his neck and her fingernails raked the smooth skin of his shoulders, he gave a snarl that matched the dark, lean, leopard-like ruthlessness of him.

"You little hellcat!" His hand gripped her by the hair and he forced her teeth and her nails out of his flesh. "You asked for this, not I, and you are going to get what you seem to be after, a reason for hating me. I wonder why you need that, *cara*? Were you afraid that if I were tender, you might like it?"

"Tender?" she choked. "You couldn't be other than arrogant with any woman—you must have your own way in everything, with no compromise! I came here to – Las Santanas as your wife, so things would be made easier for Dmitri, but you couldn't—it would be beneath your pride and dominance to let me alone. You know I don't want you—in that way!"

"Very probably you don't want any man—in that way," he mocked her, and there was a sudden ripping sound as he tore the pyjama jacket from her body so the buttons popped and her skin gleamed like pale silk in the dusky gold light of the bedroom. "You came to the castle of Santigardas, not to a convent, *menina de nieve*. You are now married to a Spaniard, and there are none of those vapid in-name-only relationships in this country. Today in church, *mi mujer*, you took my ring, my name, and now you take me!"

"Brute!" she gasped, and burned with absolute torment as his eyes ran over her skin, which was only fractionally less white than the pillows against which he held her, both hands painfully gripping her and his teeth glinting as she struggled with him, so that her body brushed his and she felt the smooth steely warmth against her, and saw as in a nightmare their combined shadows thrown upon the white walls of the room.

"No . . ." It was a sob and a plea, a broken little moan as his body crushed hers and his arms locked themselves around her so that she was made helpless, and could only toss and turn her head until she was blinded by her own hair. And all the time she could hear him softly laughing at her, jeering at her for being unable to match his hateful strength and arrogance.

"If you keep this up, *menina*, you will be a mass of bruises in the morning, for you have that kind of skin, haven't you?" His lips brushed her so she felt the edge of his teeth. "And look how your pale hair shimmers against you, like a skein of raw silk. Little fool, not to know that your indifference might have bored me; that I might have shrugged and turned away from cold passivity. But I like a fight . . . I like very much the little fury you are tonight."

He drew a little away from her so he could look at her. "Your eyes are those of every woman who ever fought against this—they blaze golden in your strange little face, half catlike and half nunlike ... *Santo Dios,* we'll find out now what you really are, shall we?"

His lips were against her body . . . a flame running over her skin . . . when abruptly a hand pounded the door on to the gallery. "*Señor!*" The voice was imperative. "Please come to the apartment of the Condesa! She is taken ill!"

154

The rest of that night—her wedding night—passed strangely for Altar. The Conde had risen, snatched a robe from his own room, and left her there on the rumpled bed, her hair wildly tangled across the covers, her arm flung protectively across her bared skin.

He had not returned, and in a strange, half-exhausted mood she had risen from the bed in a while and concealed her torn pyjamas at the bottom of a drawer. Then she had put on another pair, smooth, chaste, unrumpled, and had combed and plaited her hair at the mirror, where in the glow of the silver lamps she had a look from which she couldn't drag her gaze . . . lips which had spat fury and now had a sulky set to them; eyes which had blazed and now had a sultry storminess about them. As she lifted her arms to secure her plait of hair, her young breasts made soft points in her pyjama jacket.

She stared at herself and saw visibly the shiver that ran through her body . . . she could still feel his touch on her skin, and in the opening of her jacket there was a mark of a bruise against her collarbone. She wanted to feel outraged, but curiously enough she felt . . . abandoned. From the nape of her neck down to her heels she felt the chill of a strange loneliness . . . and a longing.

She ran to the bed and with trembling hands she straightened the covers and rearranged the pillows. What, she wondered, had made the Condesa ill? Was it a genuine upset, or had it affronted her cold and bitter dignity to think of Estuardo with his young wife, alive and vibrant with life, while Gregory, her idol, lay in that sleep from which there was no awakening?

Altar couldn't sleep and she wandered to the balcony where she stood in the cool darkness and breathed the scents of the patios and gardens, wrapped in velvety shadows. She knew that the Condesa's apartment was in a front wing of the castle so she couldn't see any lights or the flurried movements of people in a state of anxiety. She thought abruptly of Dmitri and went into the nursery to see if he had been awakened.

"My pet, you should be in dreamland!" There he lay with eyes wide open in the soft glimmer of the night-light. When he caught sight of her he held out his arms to be cuddled and at once she bent over him and lifted him into her arms. She rocked him and murmured to him, but ten minutes later he was still awake, and because she was almost rocking on her own feet as the combined emotional upsets of the day, and night, swept over her, she took Dmitri to her own bed, and her first night at the castle was spent holding in her arms the child of her husband's brother.

Sunlight was in the room when she awoke, to find herself cradling the baby while a tall figure stood at the bedside looking down at her, a cup and saucer held in his hand.

"There was really no need to bring Dmitri to your bed," the Conde drawled, a sardonic lift to his brows as he regarded her plaited hair, the pink-striped pyjamas which had replaced those he had torn, and the way she held Dmitri pressed to her heart. "I have been with Madrecita for most of the night, and it really would have been anti-climax, my dear, to have returned to try and recapture that wild and enchanting picture of you which I carried away with me. This morning you look—*Madre de Dios*, how different, like the plain side of a coin that has a surprisingly complex side to it."

"How is your grandmother—was it anything serious? I—I stayed in my room, for I didn't want to be in the way. I know she doesn't like me, but I hope she's now feeling a lot better?"

"She will eat lobster *pâté*," he said, and the aroma of coffee drifted to Altar as he placed the cup and saucer on the bed-table. "It gives her a devastating heartburn which, at her time of life, isn't pleasant and can be frightening. She is now restful, and swears adamantly that she will never eat lobster again—which she will, of course. It is the things that trouble us the most which we find ourselves unable to resist. How was your night, *mi mujer*?"

"I slept well," she rejoined. "Dmitri was awake, so I brought him to bed with me rather than leave him alone in the nursery. I—I didn't know how serious your grandmother's upset was and when these things happen at night—well, the atmosphere always seems a bit melancholy. I'm glad to hear that the Condesa is now all right and that it was nothing too bad."

"No, she is quite recovered—I'll take the boy while you drink your coffee. Maria can see to him. She's proficient young person who has grown up in a large family, so she knows how to deal with babies." He lifted Dmitri out of the warm nest of Altar's arms, and she saw his lips quirk with that slightly mocking smile of his. "It was a memorable wedding night, both of us acting nursemaid to the two people most closely bound to my brother. I begin to wonder what exactly is in store for us, *mi mujer*."

He carried Dmitri away with him, but he left Altar with the echo of his words as she sat drinking her coffee. Not only had he been clad for riding, but there had been the tang of turf on him, so she guessed he had been out early, riding beyond the castle to the high ground where the bulls roamed. He had said that she was complex, but so was he! Last night in this shadowy room he had looked a satyr intent on having his own way . . . yet the same frightening person had spent the remainder of the night quietening the fears of an elderly woman who, if she cared at all for him, kept her feelings well hidden.

Altar decided that she was never going to understand him, and she too wondered what lay in store for them. She had thought that she could leave the castle . . . walk out, with his blessing, but it wasn't going to be that easy.

Eagles, she thought, didn't let go of their prey once they had it in their grip, and she could feel something about this place gripping her, holding her. She slipped out of bed and went across the deep rug in her bare feet . . . the balcony doors were still open from last night, but this time when she stepped out on the flagging she found it already hot from the sun, and the multi-coloured bougainvillaea that draped the coping was brilliant with colour and alive with bees. She could hear them humming as she went to the part of the coping that was undraped by the flowers, and she stood there taking in the beauty of the morning, in the far distance the grey-mauve, ice-tipped peaks of the *sierra*, and below them the sweeping plains that went on and on, presenting a vista of freedom that made Altar feel a strange sense of captivity up here on the balcony.

It was wide and semi-circular and when she turned to look upwards she saw that the apartment she shared with the Conde was situated in one of the tawny-stoned towers of the castle. He had told her upon their arrival that he had always liked the towers when he was a boy; in those days they had represented a form of escape for him . . . now she could only wonder what his feelings were when he stood there and looked at the plains and the mountains that were his boundaries.

He was the *dueno* of all this, but Altar knew that in lots of ways he was less free than his own *vaqueros*, the herdsmen who lived and played hard, but who had reins less tough to hold than the man who was now responsible for a heritage he had not sought. For the sake of all this he had surrendered his freedom; for the sake of his brother's child he had married her.

She stood there silent and thoughtful, gazing over his lands that seemed boundless . . . if only she were the sort of person who could delight in mere possessions, for by marrying her the Conde had given her a life-long right to all this.

Her hands clenched the hard coping and she wished it were enough, but she knew in her heart that it wasn't . . . she looked down upon all this tangible beauty and seemed to know at last the secret of love. Love was a gift which had no tangible shape. It was just there . . . you gave it and were wrong to expect it to be returned. A gift so personal, so mysterious, so total, was given for all time, until you died.

Last night in Estuardo's eyes she had fought furiously a passion that was not love . . . biting and clawing him because he only sought from her what any other woman could have given him. Any one of those svelte and carelessly charming creatures with whom he had passed the time in the playgrounds of Europe, until tragedy had struck at his family and duty had called him home to take on those responsibilities he had never wanted.

Now he thought of passion as some form of reward, and he didn't ask for love because love had killed his brother. Altar's hands ached from their grip upon the coping as she remembered the way he had kissed her a moment before that abrupt summons to his grandmother. His fierce lips had lingered for a fraction of time that had seemed endless, and when he had drawn away from her she had seen his distorted face in the golden lamplight, the gleam of black silk as he got off the bed, the little rivulet of blood running down his shoulder when he had turned and left her.

"*Ola!*"

She gave a start at the shouted word and glanced downwards. A man was standing down there in the patio immediately under the tower windows, where a fountain splashed, coloured zephyrs caught in the sprays of water from the collision of the sunshine with the moisture. He wore a cream-coloured shirt over bark-brown slacks, open at the throat so a medal glinted there on a chain. His hair was black and inclined to wave, and he was looking up at Altar with arrantly smiling dark eyes.

"*Buenos dias*," he called up to her. "A Julieta, I see, in pink pyjamas, and very pretty, too!"

Altar stared down at him . . . Claudio? Yes, it seemed very possible, for his clothes were of an excellent cut, and though he didn't resemble the Conde in the remotest degree, he had the dark eyes of the Condesa, almost stabbing in their scrutiny; a jetty sharpness that was unsoftened by his smile.

"You are the young wife, eh? I stand under your win-

159

dow, Julieta, to apologise for taking your husband away from you last night."

So it had been he who had come to their bedroom door, but strangely enough she was unconfused. No other man than the Conde could confuse her and throw to the four winds that reserved composure which even with Amy du Mont she had learned to hold on to. Now she kept it, even clad as she was in her pyjamas, a not very glamorous figure for the cousin to catch sight of despite his compliment, and he looked the type who would pay court to anything that had the female shape.

"It was in a good cause, *señor*," she called down to him. "I am glad to hear that your great-aunt is so much better this morning."

"So you have guessed that I am Claudio, eh?" His look became shrewd as he studied her, as if he suddenly realised that she might not be so naïve as she probably looked, leaning over the balcony with her plait swinging. "I am not good with the sick, *niña*, but my cousin the Conde has nerves of steel when it comes to dealing with most situations, and if ever thrown off his high horse by anyone he soon gets his own back—as you probably know from your own experiences of him."

It seemed to Altar that he stressed those last few words and gave her a hint of what sort of behaviour she could expect from him. He probably knew from the Condesa that her marriage to Estuardo had taken place yesterday, but as Dmitri was believed to be her baby she immediately took on the aura of a persuadable female.

That belated flush stung her cheeks and she drew away from the edge of the balcony.

"Come down and have breakfast with me," he invited. "We have to get to know one another, for I'm more or less a fixture at the *lonja* attached to the castle. Come along, I know you aren't as shy as you look."

When he said that Altar wanted to refuse him, but no problem here at the castle was so easily disposed of. Claudio was in the good graces of the Condesa, and it

160

lay in the old tyrant's hands to make life bearable for Altar, and a bearable life was all she could expect if she stayed at the castle . . . and somehow it seemed her duty to stay. Dmitri loved her and turned to her as his mother, and if she ran away he would grow up with no gentle influence in his life. Neither the Conde nor his grandmother were gentle people, and a child needed that in his formative years; the security of a haven that gave and didn't make demands.

"Give me fifteen minutes," she called down to Claudio.

"Bravo! And how to you like your eggs?"

"Fried both sides, please."

"I thought only cautious people liked their eggs that way?"

"I am cautious, *señor*," she rejoined, and as she drew back into her bedroom she had the feeling that Claudio was smiling to himself and judging that she had been very incautious in her association with the Conde. Wasn't there a black-haired, bouncing baby to prove it?

Oh lord, what a situation! She made for the bathroom, peeled off her pyjamas and stepped into the shower cabinet. The panels were of the kind that were almost translucent, but she didn't think about this until a tall shadow appeared at the other side of the glass.

"*Menina*, I have business to attend to at one of the olive yards—will you be able to amuse yourself for a few hours? I should be back in time for lunch."

She gulped as she measured the length and breadth of the shadow, and she held the sponge clenched against her bare wet body as she realised that he could see the pale shape of her through the panels. How naïvely she had gone into this marriage, barely realising that the man she married would have the right to see her day and night, clothed or unclothed, in a willing mood or an unwilling one.

"Y—yes, I shall be all right." She knew that the quavering note in her voice betrayed her embarrassment . . . to this man, her very own husband, she was all indignant virtue, ready to use teeth and nails in an effort to preserve her self-possession, but to everyone else she was the very opposite. The situation had farcical shades to it, but right now she wasn't in the mood to appreciate the humorous aspects. She knew that Estuardo saw her through the panels and remembered last night he had almost possessed her slim body . . . outraged, thrashing on the bed, so white against the bronze skin of his powerful body . . . loving him and hating him for using her as a means of forgetfulness.

"Altar, come out here a moment, before I go."

It was an order, and she didn't want another exhausting battle with him. "I—I'm all wet," she said. "Could you get me a towel?"

He was holding the towel in readiness when she stepped from the cabinet and she felt the tremor in her legs as she entered the blue folds and he wrapped them around her. She wore a shower cap and her hair was tucked beneath it as she stood there, and she wasn't surprised when he suddenly smiled.

"One moment an enticing nymph, and the next a *chiquilla*. What does a man do with a girl like you?"

"I—I thought you had all the answers, *señor*."

"I thought I did," he mocked. "By now you should be a woman I could take hold of and be sure of holding, but you are still that elusive piece of silk that keeps slipping from my grasp." He reached for her and the towel slipped from her shoulders as he pulled her against his shirt and breeches.

"It could happen now, and why not?" he drawled. "But you'd hate my guts, wouldn't you, Altar, if I shattered your ideal of the perfect knight who allowed the foot of his lady to rest on his bowed neck. However, I can't live with you with a sword between us; I have to make you mine if you break every fingernail on me and loosen every tooth. Understood?"

She nodded and pulled the shower cap from her hair because it made her feel foolish. The action caused the towel to slip lower, and she gave a little shiver as his hand brushed her small damp breasts.

"You see how it is, Altar." His lashes shadowed his stunning gaze. "We are not brother and sister, and when I see this pretty body of yours I want to touch and caress and find out its secrets. Why be so afraid of life? I shan't cause you to die if I take what is mine, after all. I'm not a callow boy who will leave you begging, and pregnant. Is it that, *menina*? You are afraid there will be nothing in it for you but an unwanted baby?"

"Please—don't—talk like this." She put her head against him, for it was easier than looking into his eyes; she smelled cheroot smoke and turf on him; warm male skin and the soap he used. Oh God, her heart cried, if only he would say lovely romantic things . . . say he adored her . . . then it would be all right . . . nothing would matter except that he took her to the bed and made a woman of her. She wasn't afraid to be a woman . . . it was just hell being a girl who wanted the man she loved to love her.

"You frigid little puss," he growled, and raking his fingers into her hair he held her in the grip of subjugation as he crushed her mouth with his. Then, his face a mocking mask, he dragged the folds of the towel around her. "There, *menina de nieve*, now all that snowy virtue is covered up, along with your blushes. *Por Dios,* I really begin to think that it's going to take a miracle to make you mine, but as you said, my dear, I am inflexible when it comes to my wife. The law makes us one, not two, and I don't plan to spend my life with a woman who belongs to me in name but not in anything else. Nor do I plan to have a willing mistress tucked away in her own apartment somewhere, if that is what you hoped? It was one thing for the younger brother to play around, but now I am the Conde Santigardas and there will be no more games—of that sort!"

He stared down at her, holding her by the ends of the towel. "*Comprendo, mi mujer?*"

"That is one Spanish word that I'll never have trouble

163

with," she said. "For that I don't need a phrase-book, do I?"

He laughed, but not with that tolerant amusement of the easy-going Anglo-Saxon. His laughter was on the edge of threat, with a whisper of Satan and seduction in it. "You must soon learn Spanish, *mia*. It is one of the few languages not yet corrupted by modern-day terms. When the Condesa and I speak Aragonese, you will be listening to one of the purest forms of speech, just as it was spoken in the days of the kings and the corsairs."

"And the captains?" she murmured, with a touch of her own devilry. "Capitan Draco, for instance?"

"Ah," his eyes gleamed, "a big hen of a bird has been whispering in your ear! Well, that is a family story—"

"Am I not a member of the family?" she asked.

"Officially, one might say." His eyes swept up and down her figure in the swathed blue towel. "If you don't take care, *muchacha*, then what befell an ancestress of mine at the hands of Draco's corsairs might well be your own fate—so far I have been as patient with you as it is in me to be patient. *Comprendo*?"

"*Si, señor*." Though she smiled as he turned on his heel and swept from the bathroom, she could feel the beating of her heart beneath her own hand. So that was what had happened to a proud member of this family in which Aragonese blood mingled with that of the Scottish Highlands! Those tempestuous, treasure-seeking corsairs who had sailed in the ships of Drake had invaded a Santigardas house and found there a woman alone . . . or had she been a mere girl?

Altar swung to a mirror and stared wildly into her own eyes. She visualised the slight swagger in the Conde's walk, and that look of almost cruel recklessness that could come into his eyes . . . her heart gave a thump and she knew that long before his much-loved Scottish grandmother had married into the Santigardas family there had been a strain of foreign blood in their veins, handed down from the girl who had fallen into the hands of those corsairs.

In the mysterious way of heritage that wild strain had come down to Estuardo, and Altar's heart told her that if she continued to defy him, he would take her without mercy, as those men had taken that Latin girl.

Having been interrupted by Estuardo, it was a lot longer than fifteen minutes before Altar was ready to join his cousin Claudio for breakfast on the patio. She had dressed in cool white, a garment which had a short flared skirt and flimsy sleeves gathered in at the wrist. On her feet were attractive wedge sandals with a blue upper, fixed like a Moroccan sandal with a tab between the toes. She wore her very new rings, but no other adornment, but as Claudio rose from the cane table to greet her, there was a look in his jet-dark eyes that informed Altar that she made an impression on him . . . a different one from that of an hour ago, for now her hair was softly looped at her nape and it had a well-brushed shine to it, holding little lights that matched her amber eyes.

A certain apprehension, a tingle of excitement left from her encounter with her husband, had added a glow to her appearance . . . an almost sensuous glow that she wasn't aware of. She only knew that she was among rather arrogant and unusual people who had the power to make life miserable for her, if she permitted it. But she wasn't going to allow any such thing, and she had decided that a proud air was better than one of shyly ashamed gratitude that the father of her supposed baby had made an honest woman of her.

"I was ravenous, so I went ahead without you." Claudio held out a chair for her, and as she sat down she could feel his eyes on her hair, her dress, and the rings that gleamed on her slim hands. "But I shall be delighted to keep you company while you eat your own breakfast. I have ordered fresh coffee."

"*Gracias, señor*." She smiled faintly as she felt him staring across the table at her. "It's a very fine morning —just listen to the birds! And what delightful colours

165

they are, like tropical birds."

"They are from the tropics," he told her. "Imported into this area long ago by our great-grandfather. Imports from other lands take well in our climate, and there is no doubt that you take to it as pleasantly as the birds. Is Estuardo going to permit that I call you by your first name, or must I be formal?"

"My husband isn't that starchy," she said, and her fingers toyed with a pair of mauve orchids that lay in a shell on the table, the hearts of them so densely purple they were almost black.

"In the years I have known my cousin I have discovered him to be many things," said Claudio, watching her pale fingers against the petals of the orchids. "He's an unpredictable man, for who would have dreamed that he would marry someone like you?"

"Who indeed?" She smiled faintly. "I hope I'm not too much of a let-down, for no doubt you were expecting his wife to be glamorous and charming?"

"I don't really know what I expected—not a girl like you, somehow. You're too—how shall I put it?" His eyes searched her face, as if seeking there some hint of the experiences she was supposed to have endured—a love affair with the awesome Conde, and the birth of her son, whom she had cared for an entire year before her marriage. Altar's nerves tightened, for this cousin of Estuardo's was a man who had been around and he was looking at her with the shrewd eyes of a Lothario.

"It's being English and having fair hair," she said flippantly. "We do keep fairly youthful, despite our tribulations. Ah, here comes my breakfast tray and that fresh pot of coffee. Your Spanish sunshine is inclined to make me thirsty."

"Even though you have lived here in Spain for some time?" He quirked an eyebrow. "Estuardo said last night that you had been living in a house on the Costa de Vista Sol."

"Yes, for a time," she agreed, and her throat felt very

dry as she poured coffee into the cups. "Do you take cream, *señor*?"

"No, I like it black and sweet," he said, and he watched her as she added sugar to his cup and then handed it to him. "Altar, you have a most unusual name—almost religious."

"A whim of my mother's," she said, and it was such a relief to moisten her throat with the creamy coffee.

"You take after her, having given the boy a name so unusual—here in Spain, anyway."

"Yes," she agreed, helping herself to bacon and eggs and a slice of brown bread. "Is this in the nature of a small inquisitorial, *señor*? Am I expected to pass some sort of character test?"

He gave a laugh. "We were bound to be curious about you, Altar, for we had no inkling of your existence until the arrival of a telegraph wire informing us that Estuardo was on his way home with his wife. It came as quite a shock to the Condesa, not that it would worry my cousin to shock anyone. He's impervious to slings and arrows, as they say, but it could not have been very easy for you, having to come here to face his family. We might have been scornful, eh? The fallen angel, picked up and brushed off and with her wings restored by the good offices of the Church."

"What a cynical remark, *señor*." She ate bacon with a casual air, but he wasn't to know that she might as well have been eating blotting-paper. She had an idea that if Estuardo had know she was going to have this meeting with his cousin, he would have intervened. He had intimated yesterday that Claudio was not to be trusted . . . and here she was in possession of a secret so startling that if it leaked out there would be hell to pay. Not only was a small boy's future at stake, but she believed that a real showdown with the Condesa would cause Estuardo to walk out of the castle, and out of Las Santanas without a backward glance. He had had duty thrust upon him, and he wasn't the sort of man to accept the yoke in a placid, patient way . . . He would always rebel in his heart . . . but if a storm ever blew up and Dmitri was discovered as Gregory's son, then Altar felt quite sure that Estuardo would consign this place to the devil and take the boy somewhere, perhaps to that house on the coast of the sun, where he couldn't be hurt ever again by his own family.

"We're a proud and rather cynical race," Claudio said. "We believe in hell and are suspicious of heaven, and I must say I admire your courage in becoming one of us. Or was it the pretty title that appealed to you?"

Instead of an answer she gave him a look of quiet scorn. He smiled and touched the orchids. "What do you think of these?" he asked. "Estuardo would call them the flowers of evil—do you notice what black hearts they have?"

She nodded and remembered the trick which Claudio had played on her husband when they were boys. "Did you grow them?" she asked.

"Yes. Now and again I travel to Brazil or Chile and I like to bring back with me these rare specimens. The Condesa also has a liking for them; she and I, in fact, get along very well."

"So I have heard," said Altar. "Estuardo had more in common with his maternal grandmother, isn't that so? He was very upset when she died."

"Ah, so he speaks of his youth to you?" Claudio had again that shrewd look, as if he would dearly have loved to see beneath her limpid surface. "She was an extremely beautiful woman, and she looked after him when his mother died—has he told you that his *madre* died when he was born? She was the daughter of his *madrecita*, who took him from a baby and reared him in her house, which was in Andalusia. Very different from this castle, white-walled and Moorish, with numerous roses of all colours all over the walls. He wanted to stay there always, but she had a fall from her horse at a *feria* there and she never regained her awareness of life and passed away in her coma. He came, then, to the *castillo*, to join his brother and myself. My parents had the *lonja*, which I now reside
168

in. You would call it a lodge in England. I have made it very much mine, and you must come and visit me there, Altar."

She nodded absently, for she was busy with her thoughts, and how sad it must have been for Estuardo to lose the woman who had taken the place of his mother, there in lovely Andalusia, where the roses grew to the size of cabbages. Or so she had heard.

"Have you finished your breakfast?" Claudio was looking at her plate on which half an egg and a slice of bacon had congealed. "You don't have a large appetite, do you? Is it nerves? Finding yourself in a strange place among strangers—except, perhaps, for Estuardo, and I know that in some ways he can be—aloof."

"I—I didn't know that he never knew his mother," she said. "That was something he didn't mention."

"No?" Claudio lifted an eyebrow. "I have always believed that if Gregory—he was the elder, as you know—had lived, then Estuardo would not have married. Ah, but I am forgetting that it was for the sake of the child—your child, eh?"

"My child," she said, with a quiet firmness, for she was beginning to think of Dmitri as hers; she was becoming imbued with the Conde's proud determination that the blue-eyed boy should grow up without a scar on his name.

"He's very handsome, I understand?"

"He takes after Estuardo, naturally."

"Naturally," Claudio echoed.

He toyed with a spoon as he spoke, and then he hit it against the side of his coffee cup and it made a ringing sound that played on Altar's nerves. "You don't look like the mother of a year-old baby—tell me, was he very staggered that you had made him a father?"

"I'm not going to discuss it—it isn't any of your business." She pushed back her chair and rose to her feet . . . and then her heart bounded as she caught sight of Maria among the flowers and trees, bringing the baby to her, clad in blue and looking so utterly adorable that

Altar ran to take him, petals scattering from an orange tree and catching in her hair, so that she looked bridal rather than maternal as she took Dmitri into her arms.

"Hello, pet, are you glad to see me?" She kissed his forehead and he clutched her neck with his plump arms and wriggled against her in an ecstasy that made her heart rejoice. She knew that Maria was watching, and Claudio ... standing there a hard stare in his dark eyes. She turned to him, and with a smile she said:

"Meet my baby, *señor*. Isn't he the perfect image of his father?"

Claudio came slowly across the patio, until he was close enough to see the boy's sparkling blue-green eyes, and the little cleft that dented his chin.

"So this is the son and heir," he drawled. "Oh yes, he has the Santigardas blood in him without a shadow of a doubt—well, you're here, *chiquito*, by the grace of fate, for the Condesa always maintained that Estuardo would never permit a woman he loved ever to have a child."

"Because of his mother?" Altar murmured. "Well, life is tenacious and it makes its own rules."

"Passion," drawled Claudio, "is stronger than compassion!"

"Perhaps," she agreed, and a quick glance at Claudio told her that he had accepted Dmitri as the result of a passionate liaison ... it was she whom he could not imagine as the Conde's partner in an affair of the senses.

It was she who was still unacceptable at the castle; even with Dmitri in her arms, a little boy plainly happy to be there, a gleam of suspicion still lingered in Claudio's eyes.

"Why do you look at me like that?" she asked him.

"Because you are the type of girl for whom a man does have compassion," he replied. "And—I think—love."

"*Gracias, señor*, it's nice of you to say so."

"Is it?" He flashed a look in Maria's direction, which she accepted as her dismissal from the scene. When the girl had gone out of sight, he leaned towards Altar.

"A man could only love you, or not touch you at all. It perplexes me, *niña*, that Estuardo should touch you and not love you!"

"Oh!" She pressed her cheek to Dmitri's soft dark hair. "No one pretends that Estuardo loves me—he married me for Dmitri's sake. He wanted to correct a mistake, and you must admit that Dmitri is a lovely mistake."

Claudio frowned as he studied her, running his eyes up and down her slim body in the soft white dress, as if he found it impossible to imagine her in a passionate embrace, or even pregnant with his cousin's child.

"Do you love him?" he demanded. "Are you in love with Estuardo?"

The question struck through her body, almost as if he had struck at her skin with his hand. She had to answer him, and there was only one truthful answer.

"Of course I love him," she said. "I wouldn't be here, not even for Dmitri's sake, if I were not in love with my husband."

And the words as she spoke them were like wild birds being released in her heart . . . that was why she had married the Conde; that was her reason for coming to the castle.

She loved the man!

CHAPTER TEN

LUNCH was over and the silence and somnolence of siesta had fallen upon the castle. Shades were drawn against the sun, which was now high in the sky and shedding a hot golden light over the walls and patios, the orchards and plains.

Altar settled the baby for his nap in the nursery,

totally unclad beneath his netting except for his white nappy, and as he lay there in the total abandon and innocence of sleep she stood looking down at him, and loving him. Was it because he had those eyes that she loved him, or was it because he was just a baby and so dependent upon her? A combination of the two, she decided, and very softly she kissed him and then wandered into her own room.

The siesta habit she found a bit of a bore, and taking a straw hat from the closet she left her room and made her way downstairs. She had not yet explored, and now it was quiet and there was no one about she would take a walk about the place and get the feel of it.

The lake, she decided. It would be cool beside the water and she would follow the contours of the lake and see where they led.

Outside in the sun she covered her head with the straw hat, pulling the brim down over her eyes to shield them from the sun. The warmth struck through the material of her white dress, and she smiled a little to herself, as she thought of Noël Coward's immortal words about mad dogs and the English and the foolhardy way they braved the tropical sun, and in this region, which was in the south, she was discovering that the sun was glorious, even as the nights were plum-blue and filled with stars as big as daisies.

Far up in those hills, she thought, there would be villages, remote, almost unapproachable, with houses hewn from the living rock. It was up there that the Conde had gone and had not returned for lunch. She had been disappointed, and at the same time relieved. She had said things to his cousin that had been so personal, and at lunchtime he would have been on the watch with those canny dark eyes of his for any sign that she and Estuardo were only actors in a drama of passion. Had she not said to the Conde that people were going to find it hard to believe that she had ever aroused his passions?

She heard the bees after honeydew in the lime-tree

leaves, and the cicadas with their insistent, low whistling sound, starting as a chorus rising to a crescendo and then lapsing into total silence as they clung, unseen, to the garden trees. Cypress trees, a jacaranda in ferny leaf, tall golden cassias, mauve plumbago, satiny yellow hibiscus, the sculptured stems of poinsettias with their fiery flowers, fuchsias like tiny dancers on fire, montbretias and vanilla-scented white orchids, all of them pollinated by the bees and the humming-birds, and recognized by Altar because of that flower book she had found in the library of the blue-shuttered house on the Costa de Vista Sol, which in his unexpected way the Conde had purchased in her name.

She came out of the trees by the water and she stood watching the bee-eaters darting in the air, making streaks of emerald and gold in the sunlight.

Altar caught her breath, for it was all so lovely, so unbelievable that she was actually here and could regard this world as her very own. A sheen of purest gold seemed to hang over the lake, and her eyes held a wonderment and a pensiveness as they gazed from under the brim of her hat, that gold light trapped in them, giving them a jewel-like quality in the inverted heart of her face.

She turned from this vantage point to gaze at the castle, a gracious, petrified dream as it stood there in the sun, showing no outward sign of the travails its occupants had known in the many years it had stood and brooded upon its own reflection in the waters of the lake. Enchanted and yet real; a place to love and to fear, for those towers represented not only protection for the occupants but their captivity as well.

The Condesa sought her moments of escape in the domed flower house, among the collection of tropical plants brought back to her from his travels by Claudio. The Conde sought his in those hills, on one of the handsome mounts from his stables.

And now it was her turn . . . hers, to find somewhere of her own, where she could be alone when the melancholy of being unloved struck at her.

It was strange to think that the Castle of the Golden Towers should harbour a family divided, without that shining strand of love's gold to bind them firmly together, sharing their tears, and their joy. Altar's heart ached as she gazed at this place that was to be her home . . . home it could never be, for too much pride held its occupants apart; too much passion had been spent in fierce words and the clash of loyalties. Altar sensed that the Condesa had come here as a reluctant bride, and she knew that as a boy of sixteen Estuardo had come here with grief in his heart. Only Gregory had seemed content—until love had called him away, and left his grandmother embittered, and his brother in charge of a castle that could never replace for him a Moorish house of white stone and rose-encrusted archways.

A castle of passions, thought Altar, and there seemed no hope that it could ever be a castle of love.

She wandered by the lake until all at once she came to a slim, timber-built bridge, almost a catwalk, across the water to one of the nearer islands. She stepped upon the planks a little warily, but they held firm and within ten minutes she was stepping off at the other side, rather hot and breathless from the sun and glad to find herself under the long shading strands of green willow and golden cypress, with a path running at an angle among them, which she followed without hesitation, glad of the coolness after the heat on the bridge.

Midges danced in the rays of sunlight that came through the trees, but she had already learned from Amy du Mont to wear a protective cream in these places where the sun was gold and the water was blue, but where the bite of a tiny insect could be venomous. Nothing was ever moderate in Latin lands, Amy had always said. Altar brushed aside a long tress of willow and a smile came and went on her lips. Avoid the sun, avoid the insects, and avoid the men; those had been Amy's dictums with regard to her companion. Not because she had a girl's welfare at heart,

174

but because sunstroke, a bite, or a man, might upset her own routine and self-indulgent way of life.

It was strange for Altar to realise that she would be unlikely to ever see Amy again . . . was she liking it in Vienna, and had she found someone else to fetch and carry for her? How amazed she would be; how bitchily amused that Altar was now the mistress of a castle: the wife of a man who would have been a handful for even a woman of the world.

The trees thinned, the sun struck warm again, and Altar caught her breath with surprise and delight, and banished instantly were all thoughts of Amy and a way of life that no longer touched the frightening magic and wonder of this marriage to Estuardo Santigardas de Reyes.

What confronted Altar was a *caseta* of chartreuse stone, set here in solitude among the trees, its roof shingled and encrusted with a mass of blue-flowered vines that had grown up the walls and partly covered the cottage with the petalled stars. Jasmine, she realised. The seeds dropped here from the feet of birds, which had quickly taken root in the leaf-mulched soil and grown over the years into that lovely, living mass of petals and foliage.

Secluded, mystic, untouched, the *caseta* seemed to stand in this lonely clearing as if it had waited for Altar to come and find it. She went forward and peered in through the tiny panes of glass and though there was dust on them she could make out the interior, which seemed to be a single room with furniture in it; a sort of doll's house, a hideaway, a shelter from possible storm.

It was irresistible, and with bated breath Altar tried the timber door and found that the handle turned back and forth but wouldn't yield. She was locked out of this delightful place and she just had to get inside. She studied the doors and the windows and walked all the way round the *caseta* to see if there was a way in. It was locked, but being quite a distance from the castle it surely wouldn't be the kind of place to which any member of the family carried a key. No, the key was here somewhere, kept in hiding in case someone fancied an idle hour alone here, or rain suddenly struck and they needed to take shelter.

Where did people hide keys? Under mats, in pots, or on the ledge of a window? After all, there was nothing of value here, for the furniture she had glimpsed inside was of the cane variety, with a few cushions scattered about, and a table with books on it

She hunted for the key, and found it, tucked inside a tiny shrine attached to the east wall of the *caseta*, a miniature Madonna and Child inside, the blue print faded off the robes, and a tiny bunch of gentians dead at the tiny china feet.

"May I?" Altar murmured, as she withdrew the key from the shrine. "I'll do no harm to the little house—I shall just sit there quietly and think."

As she unlocked the door she had a momentary sense of invading something private, and then she stepped inside on the rush matting and the *caseta* was so cool, and the deep cane chairs so inviting, that she told herself not to be a little idiot. Whatever ghosts were here they were pleasant ones, for the very fact of the little shrine testified to that.

Altar closed the door behind her, leaving the key in the lock so she would know it was there. She glanced around and saw from the layers of dust that no one had been in here for quite a time. She put out her hand and broke the strands of a web binding a coloured jug to a table lamp; the sort in which oil was used, with a blue globe. The colours of the cushions had faded on the cane lounger, and the edges of the books had begun to darken.

What a pity for a place like this to be nelected, she thought, and she shook out the cushions on the lounger and sat down to study the room and to tell herself, still with that sense of unreality, that as the wife of Estuardo she had the right to this cottage whenever she wished. She could have it cleaned out and put to use again. She could have the rush matting replaced, hang flower prints on the walls, which a fresh coat of white paint would make dazzling. She could send away for some of her favourite English novels, bring flowers here, roses, and put them in the coloured vases. In no time at all the place would look really inviting and she could use it as her own special hideaway. No one would mind, Estuardo least of all.

Her fingers clenched the brim of her straw hat, which she had taken off, for in a while, when his curiosity about her had worn off, he would begin to forget that she was a part of his life. How could it be otherwise when he didn't love her? He wanted her . . . he had said so, but that was only to assert his possessiveness; to have what was his by right of the legal formalities.

She stared at her own hands, on which gleamed the rings he had put there. The rubies were deeper than flame or wine and were like drops of blood . . . she gave a little shiver, for it would have been a passionate pain and pleasure to know herself the beloved bride of Santigardas. As it was there was only pain in the knowledge that she belonged to a man and must give herself to him. Give . . . or be taken, for that was what he had threatened, and there was in his nature a vein of ruthlessness too deep for idle threats.

She laid her hat on the side table and swung her feet to the lounger. She felt enervated all at once by the sun and by the broken sleep she had had last night. She had kept waking to ensure that Dmitri was all right, and anxiety for the Condesa had mingled with a certain apprehension that Estuardo would return to her.

Her eyes drooped and she allowed her head to rest against a cushion. She would have a little rest . . . it was so quiet and peaceful here . . . her eyes closed, her thoughts grew less tormented and very gradually her body relaxed.

Altar slept with the suddenness of a child whose emotions had been on edge for hours. Her lashes lay still and dark on her cheeks, and her hair spread its brightness against the faded cushion-cover. One of her sandals slipped to the matting, but she didn't stir, and as she lay there, lost to her bewildering world for a while, a small ray of sunlight edged in through a windowpane and sought contact with the rubies on her slim hand. They flared with flamy colour, beautiful against her young pale skin.

She awoke several hours later to a room in total darkness, and with a little cry she sat up and her heart bounded with fear. Where was she . . . oh God, everything was as dark as pitch! She flung out a hand in panic, as if seeking a bedside light, and there was a shocking crash and a splintering of glass, and at once she was fully awake and conscious of where she was.

She had fallen asleep in the *caseta*, and from the sound of that crash she had knocked to the floor and broken the oil-lamp. Well, all she could do for the next few minutes was sit here and let her eyes get accustomed to the darkness . . . how horribly dark it was . . . dark as it could only be in the south when the sun went down and night took toll of the day. But outside in the sky there would be starlight, and she wanted so much to see the stars that she stood up without realising that one of her sandals had fallen off while she slept.

A sharp cry of pain broke from Altar as she stepped upon a piece of shattered glass . . . she felt the blood at once, running from her foot into the matting, and her panic at the darkness mingled with that immediate fear that strikes at the heart when blood is spilled. She sat down again and because her handkerchief was far too small to make an adequate bandage she took a shaky breath and ripped her dress, tugging and pulling and feeling all the time the stinging pain of her foot and the moist stickiness of the blood on her toes.

Why, oh, why did she lack that essential poise that made it impossible for some women to get into the predicaments that she got into? She finally managed to tear off a piece of her dress—thank goodness for the white cotton shift she had changed into after lunch, a dress from her companion days and inexpensive—but as she wrapped the material around her foot she wondered how she was going to creep back into the castle without being observed. The hall would be brightly lit and the servants would be about, and it would be rather mortifying to be seen like this, tousled, torn and bloody. Latin people were volatile; they didn't have that calm and unruffled acceptance of these minor upsets that English people had. If she was seen there would be such a fuss made that one might think she had lost a toe . . . she didn't want any fuss. All she wanted was to get to her bedroom and there be able to bathe the foot in privacy and cover the cut with a piece of medicated adhesive.

Gingerly she sought about for her sandal and just about managed to put it on, then having grown a little more accustomed to the darkness she made her way to the door and opened it. At once she heard the rustling of the trees and the rather mysterious calls of the night birds. But it was an intense relief to see the stars, and after relocking the *caseta* and returning the key to its hiding place, she set out, hobbling slightly, on the path that led to the lake.

Strands of willow brushed her face and her hair, and a couple of times her heart came into her throat as great pale moths flew towards her and seemed as if they would entangle their wings in her hair. Mistress of the castle! What a joke ... what a laugh! She felt sure the fates were laughing as she hurried home, looking as if she had been dragged through a hedge backwards!

It had to be, of course, for nothing ever happened to her that was moderate. Nothing! She lost her dearly loved father in a fire. She became the companion of a woman of immoderate selfishness. And to cap it all she married a man for every reason except the one that mattered—but it was his name she cried out as she misjudged the exact location of the plank-bridge in the darkness which the willows and the cypress trees intensified, shutting out the glimmer of the stars.

As she went plunging into the cold water in the dark, her husband's name was half a scream and half a despairing certainty that she was never going to see him again. Then came the shock of the water and the splash she made, plunging in with a gasping cry. Instinctively she grabbed at the long tough willow tresses that hung down the bankside and floated on the water. She clung to them as if to a rope, while the water sucked at her, smelling green and primitive, and splashing into her nostrils and her eyes.

She screamed again, this time with sheer temper, and there on the bridge above her came the clatter of hooves and the weight of a horse shaking the planks so hard that they seemed as if they would give way.

Estuardo?

She struggled to hold on to the willow-whips, while the water dragged at her as if to pull her beneath its green surface. She took a deep choking breath. "Estuardo . . . please . . . I'm here!"

Afterwards she thought it a good thing that she didn't understand more than a few words of Spanish, for she felt sure the language that her husband used was straight out of the bullrings and wine cellars of Madrid and Seville combined. He lay on the bank in the mud and the nettles and pulled her from the water like a fish on the end of a line, and all the time he cursed in Spanish, and the words had the edge of diamonds and steel and the redhot pincers of the Inquisitors.

He dragged her, wet, weeping and shivering, up the bank to where his horse shook its bridle and puffed its nostrils at the green smell of the water as Altar was lifted into the saddle. She clung there to the hard edge of the saddle as Estuardo swung up behind her, closing his damp strong arms around her as he took the reins.

"I will not ask a single question right now," he said crisply. "But, by heaven, I shall expect a few answers later on, when they've bathed you, dried you, and spooned some

180

hot soup into you!"

That gallop home was the strangest experience of Altar's life, the planks of the bridge rocking under the supple prancing of the horse as he was urged to speed across to the other side. The wind blew against her soaked body, and rivulets of water ran from her hair. Both her sandals were gone, along with the bandage she had tied about her foot. The coldness was such that she no longer felt any pain . . . all she was acutely aware of was the hard thrust of Estuardo's chest muscles against her shoulder-blades, the strength and feel of him, more real than anyone else in her life.

Once she had thought of him as a black knight . . . now he was her knightly rescuer, not the shining sort, with a saintly soul, but a man who did what had to be done with speed, matador language, and no tiresome lecture. They galloped in under the great archway of the castle and there in the courtyard he slid from the saddle and lifted her down, carrying her wet and shaking into the patio that led into the hall.

When the bright light of the chandeliers fell upon them, Altar wanted to bury her face against him and not be seen. But the servants were there, and also the Condesa, with a dark lace mantilla over her silver hair.

"*Santa Maria*!" It was she who saw the blood all over Altar's foot, for the cut had started to bleed again. "What has happened to the child?"

"The good *Dios* alone knows," her grandson rejoined. "Diego, I want two of the girls up in the *señora's* room at once. I want a hot bath for her, hot towels, and hot soup. In the meantime bring the *coñac* and a glass!"

He took the stairs two at a time and Altar's head seemed to whirl, so that she did have to press her forehead against him.

"You little fool," he said roughly. "What game have you been playing?"

"Things just happened," she said weakly. "I—I didn't ask for any of this—it's like a curse on me, because of all

181

the lies—"

"Hush—you mustn't speak like that." He carried her into her room and across to the bed, and after he had laid her down he switched on the lamps. "What lies are you talking about, eh?"

"Y—you know—" She winced as he took her foot in his hands and studied the cut that was now stinging sharply again.

"*Gran cielo*, there is glass in this! In the name of the saints how did this happen?" he demanded.

"I—I broke a lamp—in the *caseta*—"

"So that is where you have been—lie still and don't wriggle about like Dmitri having his toes tickled. Hold quiet, *pequeña*, for I can't let this little dagger of glass remain in your foot—there, it is out! Done! You feel faint?" He leaned over her, twisting the bedcover around her foot as the blood ran freely again. "It must bleed and then it will be clean, for that water by the lake edge is by no means clean."

He stared down at her white face as he spoke, gazed deep into her amber eyes that held pain, and the pensive wonderment of finding herself alive and with him—despite everything.

He leaned lower, resting on his elbow above her lax body in the torn and stained cotton dress that clung wetly to her body. "What lies?" he murmured.

"Our marriage—the pretence—everything—"

"Pretending what, *mia*?"

"Th—that I ever had—your baby."

"As if I'd ever give you a baby and risk losing you!"

The words were distinct and yet softly rough as velvet. The words were as real as a lash sting, and yet unreal as a dream. Her amber eyes saw him, her slim wet body felt him, the lake water and the blood from her foot were on his person. A tremor shook her, and at once the strange shimmer was gone from his eyes and he glanced towards the bedroom door.

"I will take the *coñac*." He held out his hand for the

bottle and the glass. "To the bathroom, *niña*, and quickly run the hot water, for this wife of mine is shivering out of her skin."

The two young maids dashed past the bed to the bathroom, but Altar caught a glimpse of dark and inquisitive eyes as Estuardo poured some of the brandy into the glass and made her sit up to drink it. "This will put a little warmth back into you," he said. "Come, you will not refuse it! If you swallowed any of that lake water, then this Spanish brandy will kill the germs—enough Spanish brandy is enough to kill a man!"

She obeyed him and drank from the glass, tears stinging her eyes at the fiery strength of the spirit. "Y—you must have some," she gasped. "You're awfully wet yourself."

He took the glass and drank the rest of the brandy from the exact spot where her lips had been. She stared at him—her body was telling her strange things that her heart didn't dare to believe. She saw an angry red mark against his throat and before she could stop herself she had reached out and touched it. "You've been stung by something," she said, and under her fingers she could feel his warm skin and the humming of a pulse.

"Desperately stung," he said, and his teeth glimmered as he reached up and pressed her hand into his throat, holding it there. "Nettles—and something else that won't fade away. *Dios*, that scream of yours, and the splash! We wondered what the hell had become of you, and then I thought of the lake—how did you come to fall in? But no! Don't tell me anything until you have soaked in the bath—"

"You must also have a good hot soak," she said. "You will?"

"Indeed!" He glanced down at his shirt, mud and blood-stained, torn from the brambles, as his flesh was. Torn and stung—with a little incoherent cry Altar leaned forward and kissed his shoulder through a rent in the white material, where his skin was raw from a scratch, and warm against her lips.

183

"You have never kissed me before," he said quietly. A waiting quiet, like that before the eruption of a storm. Altar heard that in his voice, and she drew hastily away from him, sliding off the bed before he could stop her, and then stumbling, forgetting that her foot was wrapped in the coverlet. He leapt quickly and had hold of her. His hands pressed her against him, from her hips to her wet golden hair.

"Why?" he demanded. "Why did you kiss me—like that?"

"Y—you pulled me out of the water." Her words were muffled against him. "Didn't you?"

"It feels as if I did." His hands ran strong and feeling down the slim curves of her. "So, a polite kiss of thanks, eh?"

"Yes—No!" she cried, as he caught her by the wet pennant of hair and jerked back her head so he could look down into her eyes. For a long, long time he looked down into those big, amber, unchildlike eyes. How could she ever feel a child again when her body, that was pressed so closely to his, was letting her know that she was a woman!

"You must have your bath." He lifted her and carried her into the bathroom, where the young maids were waiting to take care of her.

"Treat her gently," he said to them. "She is the only wife that I have. Let her soak for about twenty minutes, then put her to bed—I shall come later to see how she is getting along."

With these words he sat her down on the bath stool, and a moment before he swung on his heel and left her, that shimmer of dangerous promise was back in his turquoise eyes.

She was drowsily at rest in the big bed, freshly made, crisp and cool, feeling like heaven to her spent body. Her foot had been attended to and though it still throbbed, she was only distantly aware of the soreness. She had

184

seen Dmitri after a delicious bowl of broth had been brought to her, and had played with him for a little while, until Maria had taken him away to the nursery.

Now she was alone in the soft golden glimmer of the lamps, and she could feel the soft beating of her heart.

Her heart that turned in her breast as the adjoining door opened and Estuardo came into the room. He wore a dark silk robe over light silk pyjamas, and he came to the bed and sat down beside her, and all he did for several minutes was to look at her, letting his eyes stray slowly over her brushed hair, her young inverted heart of a face, and her pale neck in the lacy scoop of her nightdress.

"You look very pretty," he said softly. "Are you very tired?"

She slowly shook her head, then held out her arms to him. They closed about his neck as he bent over her, and a little arching thrill ran through her as his lips caressed her soft young neck, and then travelled to her mouth, her eyes, the velvety lobe of her ear.

"We have memorable ways of discovering each other," he whispered into her ear. "Dare I hope, *guapisima*, that you love me—a little?"

"I love you, *guapo*, a lot," she replied, twisting her head so that his lips were on hers again. They kissed, endlessly, and then she found the courage to say what had to be said.

"One day, Estuardo, let us have a real baby of our own —please!"

"No!" His face twisted. "You are too young—there is no need—"

"There is, *mi hombre*, if you really care about me." Her arms gripped his neck and she spoke against his flesh. "I never knew what it was to be really alive until I met you—I want to know what it's like to be utterly alive. Do you think that a woman counts the cost when she gives herself to the man she loves, and is loved by? I wanted so much for you to love me when you—when tonight came. I want to be part of you—now. I want what

185

you are to be part of me."

She let her head fall back against the pillows and she looked into his eyes, and she smiled, unafraid to face the world and whatever the dragons lurking in it. "I know about your mother, my dear, but please don't deny me. Let me know what it's like to have a baby of my very own."

She felt him shudder when she said that, and then with a groan he took her completely into his arms. "If I lost you—"

"You won't," she said. "I'm very tenacious of life—look how I hung on till you came like my black knight to my rescue."

"Black knight, indeed." He pressed his lips to the tiny mole against her temple. "When you screamed, *queridisima*, I felt as if a knife went through me, to my soul itself. I knew then—I was no longer unsure of what I felt for my strange and curious little cat. I knew!"

"You used the most fearful language," she half-laughed. "I could understand it without understanding a word."

"*Si*, you will often make me swear—but more often you will make me feel—ah, so good." He laid his head beside hers on the pillow, and like that, arms tightly about each other, they fell asleep, for there was tomorrow, and all the tomorrows, for the loving.

Mills & Boon
Best Seller Romances

The very best of Mills & Boon
brought back for those of you
who missed reading them when they
were first published.
There are three other Best Seller Romances
for you to collect this month.

DANGEROUS RHAPSODY
by Anne Mather

Emma's job in the Bahamas was not as glamorous as it seemed
— for her employer, Damon Thorne, had known her before —
and as time went on she realised that he was bent on using her
to satisfy some strange and incomprehensible desire for
vengeance . . .

TEMPORARY WIFE
by Roberta Leigh

Luke Adams was in love with his boss's wife, and it was essential
that their secret should remain a secret — so Luke made a
temporary marriage of convenience with Emily Lamb. But
Emily didn't know Luke's real reason for marrying her . . .

MASTER OF THE HOUSE
by Lilian Peake

Alaric Stoddart was an arrogant and autocratic man, who
had little time for women except as playthings. 'All women
are the same,' he told Petra. 'They're after two things and two
things only — money and marriage, in that order.' Could Petra
prove him wrong?

If you have difficulty in obtaining any of these books through
your local paperback retailer, write to:

Mills & Boon Reader Service
P.O. Box 236, Thornton Road, Croydon, Surrey, CR9 3RU.

Mills & Boon
Best Seller Romances

The very best of Mills & Boon Romances
brought back for those of you who missed
them when they were first published.

In April
we bring back the following four
great romantic titles.

DARLING JENNY
by Janet Dailey

Jennifer Glenn, smarting from a disastrous love affair, had
taken herself off to the skiing grounds of Wyoming to 'get
away from it all' and lend a hand to her busy sister Sheila at
the same time. She never expected to fall in love again so soon,
and certainly not with the man who was himself in love with
Sheila!

THE WARM WIND OF FARIK
by Rebecca Stratton

Linsie Palmer was a very new journalist on her very first assign-
ment. The disturbing Celik Demaril was the man she had to
interview. When he refused to see her Linsie decided to stow
away on his yacht — with disastrous consequences!

THE MAN AT KAMBALA
by Kay Thorpe

Sara lived with her father at Kambala in Kenya and was
accustomed to do as she pleased there. She certainly didn't
think much of Steve York, the impossible man who came to
take charge in her father's absence. 'It's asking for trouble to
run around a game reserve as if it were a play park,' he told
her. Was Sara right to ignore him?

FOOD FOR LOVE
by Rachel Lindsay

Amanda could see problems ahead when her boss, Clive Brand,
began taking serious interest in her, so she changed her job.
And found still more problems in the person of that mysterious,
maddening man, Red Clark!

The Mills & Boon Rose is the Rose of Romance

Every month there are ten new titles to choose from — ten new stories about people falling in love, people you want to read about, people in exciting, far-away places. Choose Mills & Boon. It's your way of relaxing:

March's titles are:

GREGG BARRATT'S WOMAN by *Lilian Peake*
Why was that disagreeable Gregg Barratt so sure that what had happened to Cassandra was her sister Tanis's fault?

FLOODTIDE by *Kay Thorpe*
A stormy relationship rapidly grew between Dale Ryland and Jos Blakeman. What had Jos to give anyone but bitterness and distrust?

SAY HELLO TO YESTERDAY by *Sally Wentworth*
It had to be coincidence that Holly's husband Nick — whom she had not seen for seven years — was on this remote Greek island? Or was it?

BEYOND CONTROL by *Flora Kidd*
Kate was in love with her husband Sean Kierly, but what was the point of clinging to a man who so obviously didn't love her?

RETRIBUTION by *Charlotte Lamb*
Why had the sophisticated Simon Hilliard transferred his attentions from Laura's sister to Laura herself, who wasn't as capable as her sister of looking after herself?

A SECRET SORROW by *Karen van der Zee*
Could Faye Sherwood be sure that Kai Ellington's love would stand the test if and when she told him her tragic secret?

MASTER OF MAHIA by *Gloria Bevan*
Lee's problem was to get away from New Zealand and the dour Drew Hamilton. Or *was* that her real problem?

TUG OF WAR by *Sue Peters*
To Dee Lawrence's dismay and fury every time she met Nat Archer, he always got the better of her. Why didn't he just go away?

CAPTIVITY by *Margaret Pargeter*
Chase Marshall had offered marriage to Alex, simply because he thought she was suitable. Well, he could keep his offer!

TORMENTED LOVE by *Margaret Mayo*
Amie's uncle had hoped she would marry his heir Oliver Maxwell. But how could she marry a maddening man like that?